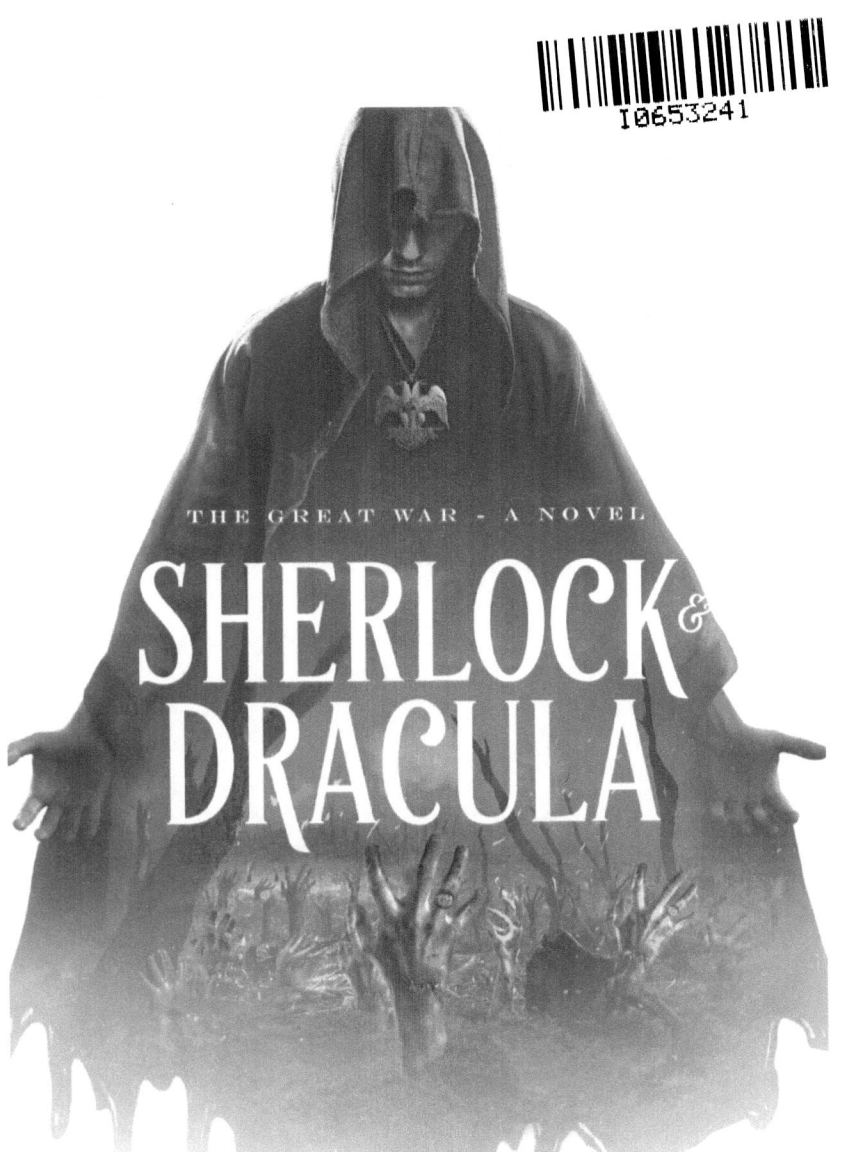

THE GREAT WAR - A NOVEL

SHERLOCK& DRACULA

KEV FREEMAN

SHERLOCK & DRACULA

THE GREAT WAR

A NOVEL

By

Kev Freeman

ISBN: (e-book): 979-8-9866630-8-1

ISBN: (paperback): 979-8-9866630-9-8

ISBN: (hardback): 979-8-9918889-0-5

PREFACE

We waited for dawn. Clements, the Innkeeper withdrew from the group and returned to the Impy without uttering a word or glancing at his rival, who sat with Marie on his lap. The Innkeeper was relieved that his wife had been saved but deeply disappointed with the realization that his marriage would be no more.

The blacksmith and his son gathered sticks and logs to construct a campfire, which, once lit, we sat beside until a chorus of birds informed us that it was time to venture inside the caves again. We all hesitated at the thought.

"Lestrade, if you would, please visit the churches in the village and return with the Monsignor and Rector thereof. We will require their assistance in rendering what we may find harmless."

Lestrade made no objection and climbed into the blacksmith's wagon. After refilling our lanterns with oil from a barrel brought by Oldham, the wagon left to collect religious aid. Then Holmes, Hopkins, Quincey, his pup, and I reentered the caves.

As we stepped from the morning light into the darkness of the caves for the last time, we did so in a solemn mood. Although our victory had saved Marie, other victims would not find any peace after their deaths, even if their remains were later to be anointed with religious blessings.

The air inside the passages was now clear of the stench of quicklime. We traced our path back towards the cavern that held the altar, where we hoped to find the remains of those who aimed a conspiracy to harm the world as we know it.

"If we find the bodies, Holmes, shouldn't they be burned before dusk?" I asked.

"Based on our experience, I would say that yes, we would need to burn and scatter the remains, so they are finally returned to the earth without hope of any reconstitution."

"It will be a task to recover the remains though Holmes," said Hopkins.

"Maybe they are to be burned in place," murmured Quincey. Prince nuzzled against his master's side.

Eventually, we reached the point of our encounter. The light from our lanterns scattered shadows around the floor and walls, the fingers of illumination shrinking, then expanding the space almost as if we were in the belly of a giant whale. A huge black void hung over our heads. What remained of the ceiling was now nothing more than heaps of limestone rock and dust.

"It appears that they are gone, and so is their master," Holmes said, kicking against the rubble with the toe of his boot.

We all knew this would not be our final confrontation, but we kept silent, knowing the Count and his followers had bigger plans for this world.

1

UNRESOLVED

Emptiness filled the cave. We stood together with not a word spared between us. The damp, musty air clung to our clothing. Our oil lamps burned. Their flames jumped and danced. The light cast flickering shadows that sliced against the sharp limestone rock outcrops of the walls. Elongated shapes, whirling like flashing blades in a cavalry charge. I looked on with nervous energy as this dance between light and dark reflected our encounter's natural battle and foundation.

The pup shivered and listened to the rhythm of distant water drips echoing and reverberating through the tunnels around us. Quincey's eyes flittered around the space in some expectation of ambush or, worse still, the reappearance of our foe. Holmes remained still. Calmly contemplating what lay before us.

Above us, a black empty void where the vast, dark

satanic mural had been illuminated only minutes before. Holmes bent down, rummaged through the debris, and picked up a piece of the fallen limestone. He stood, raised the piece to his nose, and sniffed. A single quick intake of breath at the face of the rock. He squinted. He lowered the rock and ran a steady index finger across the crumbling painted surface.

"Hopkins, here, hold my lamp. The coating is not yet cured; see."

He directed the stone towards me as it lay balanced, face up in his palm. Our lamps flickered in unison, distorting the rendering. The impact of Holmes' finger became clear. A trough wiped diagonally across the render like a plow across a muddy potato field. A soft crust of paint spread aside to reveal the rock below.

"The imprint has smudged the coating," said Hopkins, his face in a quizzical twist.

"Yes, the image has been applied in place. Knowing that we can estimate the period of its creation."

"Your estimation then, Holmes?" I said.

"It is normal that paint of this thickness would take between one week and several months to cure. But observe. The surface of the emulsion has a skin to it. Underneath the crust, the dampness of the cave rock causes an extension of the setting time of the oil. The coating is still somewhat of an emulsion, but parts have almost fully congealed."

"For how long?"

"It appears the mural has been in prepared over a period of many months, Watson."

"Long enough for a plan to be hatched. Eh?"

"Precisely, my good man, precisely."

Our eyes continued to scan the scene. Suddenly, amidst the rubble, something glittered gold and flashed in the light of the lamps. We both glimpsed it at the same time. Holmes hurried towards the location of the reflection.

"Look, over there," I said. Before I could react, Holmes had set off toward the object. I followed a step behind.

Quincey, Prince, and Hopkins stopped their investigations and followed Holmes with their eyes. Reaching the spot, Holmes squatted on his haunches and scrabbled his fingers into the dirt. His digits shifted the rubble clear of the object. Holmes pulled a small nugget into his palm, wrapped his grip around it, and stood.

"The lantern, Watson, hold it firm," Holmes urged.

I held the lantern at arm's length above head height. Holmes directed his hand into its light and opened his fingers to reveal the object.

"A ring! It's a gold ring, Holmes," I exclaimed.

"Yes, worn by the followers of the Count, I have no doubt. This ring is a symbol of their allegiance, a mark of their membership in his coven," Holmes explained, his eyes never leaving the glinting gold.

"A marking on its top, Holmes."

Holmes plucked the ring from his right palm and held it upright between his index finger and thumb. He rotated the jewelry until the inscription caught the light. He took a deep breath and blew at the face of the engraving to clear the dust, which dislodged and dispersed in a plume of fine limestone powder. Still gripping the ring in his left hand, Holmes removed his eyeglass from his jacket pocket and placed the lens before his squinting eye.

"More light, Watson! Come closer, Hopkins," Holmes urged as he twisted the object until the amber light of the lamps caught and revealed a familiar image carved within the shadows of its surface.

"The double-headed Eagle!"

"The same symbol as we discovered at the Inn?" I asked.

"Yes, and a Latin phrase to go with it. 'OCCULTA SANGUINE'." Holmes added.

"Occulta sanguine," I mulled, running through my sparse knowledge of Latin with little response from the depths of my mind.

"It must mean the occult!" I said, peering at the ring.

"No, in this case, I think you may find its part in this

inscription is 'hidden.'

"Hidden. Then what could the word mean?"

"Really, Watson, you continue to astound me without surprise. Hidden being the meaning, not its physical presence."

I shrank back and held my tongue while Holmes continued.

If I recall correctly, 'Sanguine' in this phrase means 'by blood'.

"Ah, hidden by blood!" I blurted.

"Quite appropriate, wouldn't you say?" Holmes turned the ring between his fingers.

"A membership, then Holmes?"

"Yes, my good man. Hidden by blood, a chilling revelation of the Count's influence," Holmes added, his voice tinged with a sense of urgency. We must relay this information to Lestrade. His task is to direct resources to find this coven and its location. There is little time before Dracula makes his next move."

Holmes placed the ring into his handkerchief, wrapping it firmly before folding the bundle into his pocket. We dispersed and turned our attention to the scene. Pieces of limestone decorated with colors on their faces. The remains of the ceiling to the cavern. Oil-painted devilled imagery, the same which we had directed to crash upon Dracula's coven.

We each randomly picked pieces of painted rock as evidence of the encounter. We placed what we considered the most vital parts in our sacks to examine in greater detail back at Baker Street.

"Yet there are no human remains to be found."

"Maybe Lestrade has discovered more from his visit to the churches?" I said.

"It would seem unlikely, Watson. I suspect more is to be found between the Folly and the well."

"Then we must head to that spot as soon as we get out of this place. Quincey, Hopkins, return to the Impy and organize food for us all. The good doctor and I will venture to the Folly and join you at our earliest convenience."

We spoke no more as we left the cold of the cave and found the warmth of the morning sun breaking through the canopy. We sped up the hill past the Imperial towards Chislehurst Manor and the Folly.

"What of Napoleon III? Where is the link?" I asked.

Holmes remained silent. There was no answer to give...yet.

2

FOLLY

Like an upturned thimble, the rotund white stone edifice of the folly stood without its platform of fog for the first time this week. The sun rose like a golden orb in a clear blue sky. Bird song filled the trees, and wild rabbits skipped across the common. The darkness and death of the caves had been dissolved by life. The day was as much on the other side of the coin as you may imagine. We approached at a steady pace and noticed the opening once barred.

"The gate. It's gone, Holmes!"

"They escape."

"But where would their path take them from here?"

"I fear they have traveled to the well near St. Nicolas' Church."

"Fear, Holmes, why so? We surely have them trapped

here, in the depths. The sky is as bright as any day I have seen these past days, and their condition must urge them to remain in the dark."

"In general, you are correct, my good man. However, have we not learned of the vast labyrinth burrowing under our feet, spinning and reaching out like a spider's web. A vast network of tunnels and caves stretches under this town. I ask you, where do they end? I suspect the network carves through to a distant entry point."

"You have an idea of the direction of such?"

"Think, Watson, where is the starting point for this? The unwelcome emergence of our protagonist?"

"You mean Dracula?"

"Really, Watson. Think, man!"

"I am Holmes. If only I had a mind as sharp as yours."

"Then, the world has hope, and there may be miracles!"

Observing the frustration on Holmes's face, I thought for a while

"Then the cemetery at West Norwood"

"Yes, my good man, that is the place."

"But West Norwood must be more than nine miles distant Holmes. It will take at least three hours at a decent pace to get through the caves to reach there."

"Consider the difficult underground terrain and add another hour. I estimate the hoard of vampires will not reach the Cemetery until..."

Holmes plunged his right hand into his jacket pocket and rummaged within its contents until he withdrew his target. A pocket watch. A press on its knob flicked it open. Holmes's brow furrowed as he considered the time.

"We engaged this group some two hours since. Then our opportunity will take us to eight-thirty or nine at the latest."

"Then they are still en-route. If only we could get to that location before them, but we are out of range, Holmes!"

"We may be, but Lestrade's men could reach that point if we can get him to telegraph instructions."

We made our way to the well and church, where Lestrade was interviewing the priest and vicar. The detective sent instructions as soon as he heard of the potential point of escape. It would be three hours after our first engagement before his men reached the Catacombs at West Norwood.

The Impy was subdued when we returned to pack our rooms. Quincey and Prince sat waiting together against the window. Hopkins had returned to his station.

The few locals sitting around the bar quieted as we

entered. Clements brought our last lunch without a word exchanged between us. Enough has transpired to dispense with the conversation for now.

Suddenly, Lestrade burst into the room, his features sharpened with a look of alarm, eyes almost closed, just slits in the center of an ashen complexion.

"Lestrade, you seem in a state?"

"Holmes...I...have...news," Lestrade gasped, taking short breaths.

"Sit down, man, get your wind and take your time."

"Barman, get this man a brandy," I yelled towards Clements.

Clements returned in a flash. Lestrade, who usually did not take a drink while on duty, swiped the glass from the landlord's hand and gulped it as one. The inspector gulped, grimaced, and thumped one hand onto the table.

"They are gone, Holmes!"

"Your men did not arrive in time?"

"Conversely, my men were there well before the group emerged."

"Then what on earth happened?"

"The report I have explains how the event unfolded."

Lestrade took out a telegram, unfolded it, and placed it on the table. Holmes picked it up and consumed the contents. His expression remained stoic as the telegram passed into my hand.

"What does it say, Dr?" Said Quincey, who jumped from his seat to be at my shoulder. I read the note aloud.

"REPORT: INS LESTRADE Request Investigation: 08:35: Location West Norwood Cemetery: Dispatch 08:54: 109 SGT TRENT, 343 SMITH, 687 GREEN, 245 WILSON, 932 BOWEN NO FURTHER REPORT.

REPORT: ALERT 09:35: Location West Norwood Cemetery: Constables attacked: Dispatch 09:38: INSPECTOR 012 COLLINS, 891 SGT CAMPBELL, 351 POWNEY: Attend 09:59: INVESTIGATION: 932 found dead at entrance to Cemetery. 109, 343, 687, 245 Dead in Crypt. EVIDENCE: Notebook 932 was found at the scene. Arrive 09:17: 245, 932 set perimeter. 687, 452 investigate crypt. 932 notes a large wagon loaded with wooden crates. 245 reports raised voices and muffled screams from the direction of the crypt. 245 assists and does not return. 935 assists. All were found mutilated. No blood on the scene. No other persons present. The wagon was not present.

10:35 ONGOING: Dr. WESTERN in attendance report forthcoming."

"They were all murdered," said Lestrade, "I sent them to their deaths!"

"This is not on you, Inspector. There is only one shadow here," said Holmes.

3

CHANGE

Several years had passed since our second encounter with Dracula. We needed a sight or mention of the fiend. The confrontation and escape from the cave system at Chislehurst marked its conclusion with a question mark. In our minds, the case I reported as 'Imperial,' a case involving a mysterious European connection and a series of gruesome deaths, has not been solved to the fullest extent. Matters remain open. Where did the Count and his followers escape to? What plans do they harbor? What more is there to the European connection? We were soon to discover.

After my marriage, I returned to civil practice. I had finally abandoned Holmes in his Baker Street rooms. However, I continually visited him and occasionally even persuaded him to forgo his Bohemian habits so as to come and visit us. My practice steadily increased as I lived on Queen Anne Street and worked relatively close to Paddington Station. From there I gathered a steady stream of commuting patrons.

Our engagement in complex and urgent cases in the interim meant our thoughts were taken away from further consideration of the events we had experienced. Through this time, and when I had the opportunity, during moments of pause, I took a discreet sideways glance into the face of Holmes or Quincey. I perceived the very look haunting each of us. I know these fears do not stray far from our subconscious.

The boy Quincey has grown like a weed. Now some twelve years old, he has taken the funds released from his recently declared dead parents' estate. And, upon the advice of a financial expert, one Alexander Holder, who owed a great debt to Holmes, provided advice and invested the funds in trust so they would provide an annual income for the remainder of the boy's life. This financial independence and responsibility mark a significant step in Quincey's journey to adulthood.

Quincey is a self-sufficient, bright young man. He departed the small living quarters at Baker Street some time ago to enroll at the Royal Military Academy in Woolwich, his ambition to become a military man. His comrades there have become his family. Holmes and, in particular, Mrs. Hudson were sad to see him leave, but things must move on.

The dog Prince does not leave the boy's side. The pup, I still refer to the dog as such, always accompanies Quincey. They are billeted together at the cadet's barracks at the Academy, a comfort to them and Mrs. Hudson. Quincey's bond with Prince demonstrates his growing maturity and sense of responsibility. He takes care of the dog while balancing his studies and cadet life.

Quincey visits 221B as regularly as his time learning at the Academy and playing some cue game called Snooks permits. He likes to talk shop about the art of war and its various subjects of mapping, fortification, engineering, and the part I know he and I enjoy most, the discussion of the use of the rifle and sword. He says he keeps up the cane practice and holds the kukri in storage only for emergencies.

On one of his visits in early November 1900, Quincey took to the table and spread the day's news all around. He keeps the scrapbooks filled with newspaper cuttings of strange and unusual events. The pastime is more than a hobby, as the collection proved in our reported 'Lifeblood' and 'Imperial' cases. The snips, pasted in order and held in place with liberal dollops of cow glue, became a set of evidential documents. We found these of great use during our subsequent investigations.

Holmes sat beside the fireplace's warm glow and puffed on his favorite cherry pipe. The grey emissions reflected the weather outside; a light fog swirled around the street. I paced and peered out of the window. We were waiting on our next case. I sensed there was something or someone who would soon request our assistance. "A murder in Germany," Quincey said, murmuring in a low voice as he cut the news report from the page of interest.

"I'm sure there are many," Holmes replied, removing the pipe and knocking what was left of its smoldering contents into the fire. Curled in his customary position by the fire, Prince stirred and thumped his tail thrice on the rug.

"Reported as a ritual event, Mr. Holmes. One which we have heard to be similar."

"How so?" I asked.

"A body of a young boy of about twelve was found mutilated and drained of blood."

"Drained of blood? There are many murders, Holmes, but few have such a similarity with the evidence found during our investigation at Chislehurst."

"Quite," Holmes considered for a moment, his brow furrowed, then he added, "continue with the report then, boy."

"It happened in Berlin and caused a substantial stir. After the remains were found, the local population in Prussia rioted in fear a secret group was carrying out ritual murders in town. The Military flooded the area to subdue the unrest. Thereafter, a large reward of twenty thousand marks was put up for the detection of the murderer."

"Twenty thousand marks, eh? I should say the equivalent of one thousand pounds!" I said.

"Please go on, Quincey," Holmes said after passing a disparaging glance in my direction.

"Yes sir, so it says that about a fortnight after the body was found, a worker named Masloff informed the police of hearing mysterious lights and sounds, as of crying and afterward the swift sweeping of stone. Masloff identified the location as the cellar of a local butcher. Suspects were arrested, but only Masloff was sentenced for perjury."

"The evidence then removed," said Holmes.

Quincey turned to his collection of scrapbooks and flipped the pages of cuttings, some colored yellow, which held the passage of years on their surface.

"I do recall more cases like this, Mr. Holmes."

"Then, my boy, what of the reports?"

"There is a case in Vienna. The body of a teenage girl. Here is the article. Agnes Hrnza it was. Her remains were found free of blood."

"The similarity, Holmes!" I said. Quincey flicked the pages with a swift movement of his hand, landing on a cutting several pages on.

"Then here, the bloodless murder of Tisza Ezsler in

Hungary. The report even remarks on this trail of similar ritual murders. There seems to be a design to cause outrage and fear of a hidden sect stalking the night."

"A trail through Europe. But where does it lead Holmes?"

4

CONTINUANCE

Winter turned to spring. This morning, the sky was clear of clouds. The air possessed a surprisingly calming warmth for a spring day in mid-April. London steamed, literally. Vapor rose from the cobbles and twisted upwards until it burned away into the azure hue of the heavens. The temperature was unseasonal in its warmth, as blazing hot as a summer's day.

Now free of the rooftops, the sun illuminated the day as bright as a burning lamp. I walked briskly from my surgery towards 221B. I half-wished that I had taken the opportunity to hail a hansom. Still, I refused to consider a retreat as I had already covered more than three-quarters the distance. To surrender to a horse-drawn or a new motor-driven cab would have only served to confirm my ill-thought reasoning.

I increased my pace and gathered speed to a half-run. Holmes' simple but telling telegram was delivered earlier that day to my desk. The matter, stated in only three words, conveyed an urgency.

'COME SWIFTLY. 221B.'

I maintained my pace and continued questioning why I thought a walk would be better for me than a cab. The consequence rattled around my mind. My mistake, confirmed by my respiration rate and significant perspiration, irritated me. I removed my neatly folded kerchief from its usual pocket stowage in my jacket.

I flicked the cotton square open, and, as a blur, I wiped it swiftly across my face. Between the wipes, I glanced along the street. Standing in the shadows, I noticed a figure dressed in dark long garb. He gazed in my direction, his eyes all but hidden by a cap pulled over his forehead. A shiver rolled down my spine. The man moved quickly into a side street, and I paid the event no more heed. I continued on my way. The perspiration replenished itself without any hesitation, multiplying the beads at a rate of two for each one wiped away.

It had been only two months since the passing and state funeral of our great Queen Victoria, a moment in time that left London exhausted. The town, subdued by the combination of swirling emotions and winter, moved on. Soon, the fog and cold were replaced with bustling activity.

People hurried into the new century, both literally and figuratively. The spring weather helped foster an increasing attitude of optimism. A tangible air of expectation has taken root in the town. According to reports from national newspapers, the new Edwardian era is due to begin with an uplifted national positivity.

Bodies, now free of winter clothing, scurried without delay. Workers cared only for their business. Peaked caps and brimmed hats shielded brows and eyes from a sky of such a blue that it hurt one's vision should you dare to risk an upward glance.

Remnants of flags and dark funeral morning banners flittered and scraped around the street like autumn leaves. My foot caught on a stray piece of litter. I shook it loose from my boot without missing a stride.

The paper released fluttered along the cobbles until it wrapped around the dark brown trouser leg of the man. The same man, I recognized him as such, who was following me earlier. The figure pulled at the litter and shook it off. A glint of gold caught one of his fingers and reflected in the sunlight. The man turned and departed in the opposite direction to mine. I hurried on.

In not more than fifteen minutes, I arrived at the door of 221B. Hesitating, I turned to inspect the street behind me. There was no sign of my pursuer. My imagination might have gotten the better of me.

In front of me was the solid friend of a door. and gripped the knocker between my fingers and thumb. I studied its familiar form, a comforting cold and polished metal worn from the regular visits of clients seeking urgent assistance. I rapped with some force at the weathered face of the door.

No sooner than the second beat had sounded, and with my fingers still gripping the brass, Mrs. Hudson answered the door with a flourish. The knocker fell from my hand and sounded the third rap by its own weight.

Although fully illuminated by the warm glow of the spring day, the housekeeper's face appeared ashen and drawn. A look of stoicism helped to furrow deep lines on Mrs. Hudson's forehead. A complexion which often accompanied a concern for Holmes during times of a particular perilous investigation.

"Dr. Watson, how relieved I am that you have made your way here quickly!" she said, arm outstretched as an invitation to enter. The door closed behind me as fast as it had opened.

"I hurried with some urgency," grasped the kerchief, wiped the still damp cotton across my face, and returned it as a crumpled rag to its safekeeping.

"You didn't take a cab, Dr?"

"It's hotter than I expected. I dressed for the cold."

Mrs. Hudson raised her eyebrows and gave me the motherly look of someone who thinks you should know better.

"Then let me take your coat. Sherlock is waiting for

you. Two visitors are with him—important gentlemen. If I'm not mistaken, I have seen one of the men visit before, and the other is a military man. I think the discussion brings trouble with it."

"The detective's skill is rubbing off on you, Mrs. Hudson. Be careful that you resist the urge to take up the pipe."

"That disgusting implement, I should better be removed to the asylum."

I followed Mrs. Hudson as she carried my coat draped over her arm. She ran up the stairway at a gallop, and I followed a step behind. We entered Holmes' studio after a quick tap on the door without waiting for a response.

I found the famous detective in his armchair. Facing him, the two visitors squashed elbow to elbow on the small settee reserved for new clients.

SHERLOCK & DRACULA: THE GREAT WAR

28

5

PREDICTION

Half-drawn against the bright sun, the blinds glowed a dull ochre. Flecks of dust carried small rainbows in the air. A fire blazed in the hearth. Bright orange sparks spat up the chimney and died in a last reach for life. The remaining room area was dark and silent, apart from the clock, as it ticked its steady rhythm. The visitors remained seated in the shadows. I squinted to gauge their features but couldn't distinguish their form in the darkness.

"Ah, here you are, Watson!" said Holmes, his voice booming across the room. He twisted in my direction and repositioned himself into the armchair, crossing his legs and puffing upon his favorite cherry pipe. A plume of foul-smelling smoke released and mushroomed towards the ceiling. "Thank you, Mrs. Hudson. You may leave," said Holmes.

The housekeeper huffed, coughed, turned, and slung my coat onto a vacant spigot of the wooden rack beside the door. Disgruntled, Mrs. Hudson exited with the same swiftness that she had entered.

"What is it, Holmes?" I gasped as I bent forward and placed my hands on my knees. The warmth of the day and the final gallop up the stairs had taken a toll, taking most of my wind with it. I took a deep breath. After a moment, my eyes became accustomed to the room's darkness, and the shadows revealed their contents.

"You better straighten up, introduce yourself, then sit down and get your breath, my good man. It seems the life of a gentleman is taking its toll on you."

"You suggest some urgency; is it not the case?" Wheezing, I raised myself straight, ignoring the stitch in my side, and glanced at the visitors, who, on my arrival, stood at rigid attention.

My vision had adjusted sufficiently for me to recognize the shorter of the two men. It was Lord Bellinger, twice Premier of Britain. We had met during the 'Adventure of the Second Stain,' sometime in the autumn of 1894, and not long before our first encounter with Dracula. A shiver ran down the back of my neck to each shoulder, and I gave an involuntary little wriggle.

Bellinger had changed little in appearance, and I was surprised to note that he had the same unease about him as he did during our first meeting those years ago. Deeply set beneath a furrowed brow, his eyes betrayed a glimmer of apprehension. A well-trimmed beard framed his jaw, adding an air of dignity to his countenance, while his hair, now entirely silver and showing signs of loss, spoke of the stress and strain earned through years of service. His face appeared gaunt and filled with gloom. Bellinger glanced first at Holmes, then me, and then at the other gentleman on his right side.

"It's an honor to see you again, my Lord," I said, removing my glove and striking out my hand. Bellinger grasped it with the tenacious grip of someone of authority, and we shook.

"Likewise, Dr. Watson. I fear we have grave business for you and the great detective here."

"Not for the first time, Eh?" I said with a smile. Bellinger did not return the cue.

Turning to face the other man, I concentrated on his appearance. He was six inches taller than his companion and stood upright without kink or bend. My gaze was caught by a brown leather briefcase resting against his leg on the floor. Mrs. Hudson was correct. A military man, no doubt about it. He held a top hat under his left arm and presented his right. There was a slight crack in my fingers as he squeezed firmly. I looked into his eyes. Unlike Bellinger, they were free of fear and desperation.

"Edwyn Scudamore-Stanhope, good to meet you, Dr," he said.

Stanhope's hair was showing signs of greying. He was

clean-cut and elegant. He was middle-aged, and his top lip had an impressive mustache angled upwards at its ends. In demeanor, he carried himself with a mixture of composure and urgency, his movements measured yet purposeful, like a man accustomed to command and order.

"Likewise, I hope," I returned, removing the awkward smile from my expression.

"The 10th Earl of Chesterfield, Watson," Holmes said.

"Ahh, Chesterfield," I said, hoping to imply a sense of knowledge of the man even though I had none. Holmes raised one knowing eyebrow in my direction.

"Illustrious company then, Holmes. Please take a seat, gentlemen." I continued.

It was clear that these men had not sought us out lightly. Bellinger's demeanor was heavy with a pressing concern, and the two of them sat down, side by side, on the document-littered settee. It was evident that they were grappling with information that threatened to unravel the very fabric of this world. This was a business of the most pressing importance, a matter of life and death.

The Premier's hands were clasped tightly onto the rim of his hat, now planted firmly on his lap. His eyes flitted around the room. Fumbling towards my customary position, I reached my usual chair beside the fire. Holmes stood and paced, pipe gripped firmly between his teeth until he spoke.

"Then, to business. What issues do you bring to our door, gentlemen?"

Bellinger leaned forward, his throat cleared, and he spoke with a voice that carried the weight of his determination, unwavering and resolute.

"Hmmm. We are aware, Mr. Holmes, that you have become familiar with the countenance of a man to whom violence and subversion are a way of life."

"And death," Chesterfield added with a spark of delight.

"He will, literally, stick at nothing. I should say that there is no more dangerous man in Europe."

"Or perhaps the world," said Chesterfield, with glistening eyes.

"We know of this man. You speak of. His name is Dracula?" I asked.

"Yes," Bellinger said.

"Tell us what you have," Holmes said. He turned to face both men. A look of concentration hit his face, and his brows arched.

"A prediction. An analysis of intelligence gathered by a group of our agents and published some five years since," Chesterfield interrupted.

"A prediction? You know I depend upon the facts of the matter in my investigations?"

"You need to read what we have in hand, Holmes,"

Bellinger said.

The Premier contacted eyes with Chesterfield, who removed a novel-sized book from his briefcase and passed it to Bellinger.

"This is the story of the coming war, the 'Great War', Holmes."

6

THE STORY

"Story?" said Holmes. He raised one brow to convey a depreciating self-answering question.

"More than a story, Holmes. It's a narrative, an attempt to forecast the course of events preliminary and incidental to the Great War. Our own military experts, including Chesterfield here, believe it will probably occur in the immediate future." Bellinger explained, emphasizing the significance of the narrative.

"A forecast of events. You realize the successful conclusion to my work is based on events, facts, and evidence. A forecast is nothing if it is based on conjecture alone."

"Holmes, allow us to move further into our purpose with this." Bellinger moved to the edge of the settee.

"As you ask, gentlemen. Please continue." Holmes paused, "for what it's worth."

"The report's authors are well-known authorities on international politics and strategy. They've derived material from the best sources to conceive the most probable campaigns and acts of policy, giving their work the verisimilitude and actuality of real warfare." Bellinger assured, underlining the credibility of the sources.

"So, a story, a narrative, and a report all in one, eh, Sir?"

"And facts," Chesterfield grumbled.

"You say authors. May I know their names? I presume they have greater renown than the well-known American medium Leonora Piper."

"Of course, you will find the contributors of the utmost pedigree, Holmes," said Bellinger. I know not of this medium to whom you refer."

"She predicted some time since that there would be a terrible war which would cleanse the world and reveal the truths of spiritualism."

"As I say, Mr. Holmes, our authors do not depend on the spiritual world. They were Vice-Admiral Colomb, an expert in the art of naval warfare. The war correspondent, Archibald Forbes."

"Forbes? Did he not report from Afghanistan?" I said.

"Yes, he journeyed from there to report on the Zulu War in Africa. He had quite a fiery relationship with Lord Chelmsford, I'll have you know," said

Chesterfield.

A thought caused my neck and back to stiffen, and I sat bolt upright in my chair.

"The Zulu War? Forbes was there in 1879?" I asked.

"He was the first to report on the final battle there, so I presume he would have been," Bellinger said.

"I say, Holmes, it's a coincidence, don't you think?" I asked.

"You know my position on such matters, Watson," Holmes stood from his seat and leaned against the mantle above the fireplace. "We digress. Please continue, sir."

"Colonel Maude, an expert in the value and use of artillery, a recipient of the Victoria Cross. Major-General Sir John Frederick Maurice, a renowned writer of military studies. David Christie Murray, the writer, and of course, the gentleman I have on my right."

"Murray, you say. The same writer of fiction?" Said Holmes.

"Murry has written for the Cornhill and issued a recent novel I have read part of it, 'A despair's last journey.'"

"Despair indeed."

Chesterfield moved to rise from his seat. Papers and documents crumpled beneath him as he shifted his weight. Bellinger thrust his right arm across the chest of the previously composed Earl. Meanwhile, Holmes returned to his chair and raised his eyebrows in a movement of dismissal.

"The quality of an author's works is not the question here, Holmes. We speak of facts and military intelligence." Chesterfield said.

"But isn't that all we have? A story of fiction cobbled together like a deteriorating shoe with the aid of various third-party assumptions and opinions." Holmes said.

"If that was all, Holmes, then we may be closer to agreement."

"Then you have more to tell."

"Our intelligence agencies report a gathering evil in Europe, Chesterfield if you will," Bellinger said.

"This book, Holmes, begins..."

"As you say. Book," said Holmes with an interrupting scoff typically issued in frustration at a client's stupidity.

"Holmes, please provide the man due time!" Bellinger said.

Chesterfield gripped the spine of the volume in one hand and shook it in the direction of Holmes with such force that I feared the breeze from its flapping pages would remove the pipe from its perch. The Earl's voice raised enough to convey such conviction that no man could doubt his belief in the voracity of the information he was about to relay.

"Our agents gathered intelligence from all points of Europe, Mr. Holmes. Word of mouth and witness statements all corroborate with trusted observation. It is through these various means and methodologies that we are able to develop this forecast."

"Then, please proceed, gentlemen," Holmes said, closing his eyes and gently squeezing backward into his creaking seat, which folded around his shoulders like an old leather jacket. A silence entered the room, broken by crackling as the fire spat embers from its glowing coals.

"A dark cloud emerges, Holmes," Bellinger said, his voice deep and solemn.

"Over England?" I asked?

"And the rest," the Earl added.

"Anarchists gather. They plot to destabilize the whole world. This document projects an assassination attempt on a member of the ruling class within the Balkans. We name Prince Ferdinand of Bulgaria as the likely target. But I should reveal that it is only done to protect our source and to deflect from the major power. We think it is more likely to be a member or associate of the Hapsburgs. Prince Franz Ferdinand of Austria, for example."

Holmes lurched forward, his eyes now open, and focused intently on Chesterfield.

"The Hapsburgs?" Holmes asked.

"You are on track, Holmes. We know that Germany, although its Emperor and his new Chancellor conversely assure the world, in flowery addresses from the throne and after-dinner speeches, that the peace of Europe is never more assured than at present. The truth is that divisions between the great powers are set, and opportunities for blame are ripe to be taken.

Any destabilization will lead to a conflict of such a scale that the framework of Europe is totally rewritten. We don't know yet whether for good or evil.

I'm speaking of the Great War, of which the world has been subject of constant dread for some years. The war, designed to re-adjust the Continent's balance, is much more likely to break out in the region of the Danube than on the banks of the Rhine."

"The connection then is Budapest?" Holmes said.

"Yes..." Chesterfield said and exchanged a darting look with Bellinger.

"But how on earth. Holmes?" I said.

"We will reach the answer in due course, Watson."

"Our agencies inform us of an organization that has established itself in Budapest, a city, as you say, Mr. Holmes, located on the Danube. It appears that this large organization is led by a mysterious man who is able to gather many followers at will. This man mirrors the forecast set in ink here. He is difficult to track as he steps around the town like a shadow, leaving a trail of spent humanity."

From the corner of the room, a measured voice whispered, "Dracula!"

7

CONTENTS

Our collective attention was abruptly diverted as Quincey, his figure silhouetted in the doorway, broke the silence. The hallway light cast a silvery glow around the young man, freezing us in a moment of anticipation. We leaped to our feet

The dog, Prince, pressed at his master's side before galloping forward through the tangle of our legs to slide into a heap in front of the fire. The dog's tail thumped three times as the pup slipped into a warm slumber, oblivious to the discussion at hand. Prince would later prove to be a crucial partner yet again in our investigation.

"You're referring to Dracula, aren't you?" Quincey's question hung in the air, shrouded in nervous energy.

"And you might be?" Said Chesterfield.

"Cadet Morris, sir," a hand slapped against the boy's forehead, his heels snapped together, and the salute was complete.

"This is Quincey, gentlemen. He has assisted in our battles against the Count on two occasions. He is fully aware of the situation. You may speak freely in front of him. Quincey, this is the Honorable Mr. Bellinger and the Earl of Chesterfield," Holmes said, returning to his seat.

"Gave us quite a stir there, boy," Bellinger said, returning to the settee. Chesterfield's forehead wrinkled to hold a set of parallel lines as he eyed Quiney. For a moment, I was transfixed by the precision of the furrows. The Earl took his time before joining his companion, crumpling the papers beneath him as he returned to his seat.

"I apologize, sir, I heard mention of a sect, and I associate that with Count Dracula and a conspiracy of his followers in Europe."

"Remember, young man, what is said here stays within these walls," Chesterfield's words carried the weight of secrecy, binding us in a pact of confidentiality. We had not yet suspected what depth of investigation this information would take us.

"Yes, sir."

Chesterfield returned to converse with Holmes.

"We believe, with some confidence, that this man 'Dracula' is organizing a group out of common sight with the sole purpose to strike at the weakest part of the balance of power, with a desire to light the fuse to war," Chesterfield said, twisting the left side of his handlebar mustache between the tip of his index finger and thumb as he spoke. The furrows on his brow disappeared like melting wax.

"That explains the events I witnessed earlier this year," Quincey said.

"During the days you disappeared from your barracks?" Holmes said, refilling his pipe before reaching out from his seat over the dog to light a taper from the fire. Prince ruffled, curled his snout tighter into his body, and slept on. The taper glowed a deep orange and spluttered a small yellow flame as Holmes ignited the tobacco in his pipe and puffed out a plume of acrid smoke.

"You knew?" Quincey asked, his back stiffened.

"Yes, my boy. You took a cab from Woolwich Arsenal to Paddington and, after that, a train to Windsor. Easy to monitor a cadet with a pointer dog in tow."

"It was the burial, sir."

"An interesting affair, wouldn't you say?"

"The burial?" I asked, puzzled.

"The Queen, Watson, the Queen man," Holmes said, somewhat irritated that I had formed such a question.

"Yes, Mr. Holmes, all in all, a peculiar event," Quincey said.

"Tell us then, my boy, what you observed."

"Well, we were allowed to leave the barracks to line the

streets, joining the crowd to view the funeral precession. Prince came along with me. It was a solemn atmosphere indeed, and the weather closed in with low clouds and drizzle. We all watched in eerie silence as the white satin-covered coffin pulled atop a military gun carriage passed."

Quincey paused for a moment. His face struck a tone of deep consideration, and then he relaxed as a thought passed behind his eyes. He raised his eyebrows. I had seen that look before, an expression of sadness that I associated with his recollection of his mother lying in a coffin, dressed in a white robe, in the cellar of Tower Bridge.

"I did find it unusual that the Queen had requested a white funeral," Quincey said.

"A bride's funeral!" I said.

"We followed the royal procession on foot as it traveled the distance from Victoria station to Paddington. I intended to trail the escort to Windsor for the service and the later burial. I managed to get onto the last carriage to Windsor."

"The dog still at your side?" I asked.

"Yes, we traveled together as always. The burial was planned to be two days following the service at the Frogmore mausoleum. I told no one of my plans."

"Apart from the cabby."

"Only my first destination, Mr. Holmes."

"The flame of the burning candle flickers but has only one direction of travel."

"Uh, quite so, Holmes," I said.

"But tell us, Quincey, what did you suspect?" Asked Holmes.

"Our experience at Chislehurst and the unresolved European connection between Queen Victoria and Napoleon III. My intuition led me to be a witness at the burial."

"To observe for extraneous visitors?"

"Indeed. I expected a visit from our foe or at least one of his followers."

"They may have been there," I whispered

"Then tell us of your adventure," said Holmes.

"By the time I arrived at Winsor, it was 2 p.m. I made my way to the Frogmore Estate and then to St. George's church, where the service would be held. The sky was overcast, and the air was foggy enough to allow us both to blend into the landscape. A skill you taught on many occasions, Mr. Holmes." Quincey said.

"The funeral service was an altogether strange affair. The precession of the coffin-bearing carriage halted when the horses drawing it declined to move further. There was a sudden panic. The horses broke free, rearing up and sprinting away, leaving the gun carriage stranded with the coffin attached. The horses reared in fear, Mr. Holmes. We have seen animals react similarly in the presence of Dracula."

"Quite so," I said with a shiver.

"I made my way closer to the church. Close enough to get a good sight of the coffin being carried into the Chapel. It was then I felt a hand on my shoulder. I turned and prepared to draw out my kukri."

"Dracula?" I spluttered.

"Two young women."

"Servants of Dracula!" I said.

"No, Mr. Watson, they were courtiers to the Queen. They had attended to Her Majesty in the last hours. They both were dressed head to boot in heavy black outfits, morning costumes, I presume. They beckoned me to join them as they walked behind the precession and conversed. The conversation turned to their actions to complete the contents of the coffin, something which disturbed them greatly."

"The contents? More than the remains of the Queen?" Homes asked.

"The courtiers informed me that they were instructed to install a number of artifacts into the coffin. Items known to the family and maintained in plain view and others hidden under a cushion."

"Very good, Quincey. Please continue. The contents of

the casket?"

"The maids also told me that the Queen was not embalmed, and a layer of soil or charcoal was laid beneath the corpse. That in itself caused me to wonder about the potential of a resurrection as we have witnessed with others."

"A layer of soil?" I said with a start, "he is right, Holmes!"

"We evidence, Watson."

"But Holmes, may not the evidence contained in the Queen's burial be the unresolved link between Victoria and Napoleon III? The bonds of friendship between them at Chislehurst. And the raising of the dead?" I continued.

"A weak link in the chain, Watson. Albeit I'll give you, strengthened by past encounters and the knowledge held by these men." Holmes gestured towards Bellinger and the Earl. It was the first indication

"What do you mean, Holmes?"

"Kaiser Wilhelm II, the German Emperor, was with the Queen as she died."

"A European connection, Holmes!"

"Go on, Quincey, we digress into another avenue. Detail the contents." Holmes said.

"A cast of Prince Albert's hand and his handkerchiefs and cloaks, a shawl made by her daughter Alice. The things that you would expect. All being of family connection. But there was more."

"A cast of a dead man's hand, good Lord! What more could there possibly be?" I said.

"A number of items linked to her once companion, John Brown."

"John Brown?" I asked.

"Really, Watson, have you not read any of the papers? I should think that the gossip section of the daily's would provide a sublime taste to your level of intellectual interest!"

"Hardly, Holmes. Salacious correspondence is of no concern to me."

"Only the salacious themselves then."

"Gentlemen, shall we continue? Time runs short in this matter," Bellinger interrupted.

"The contents then, Quincey?"

"A pocket handkerchief of Brown and a lock of Brown's hair wrapped tightly in her hand with a gauze wrap. Flowers were arranged so the family could not see."

"The color of the flowers?"

"White."

8

LEGEND

We saw the same white flowers during our hunt for Dracula in Lifeblood. My thoughts returned to our conversations with Van Helsing and his instructions regarding the garlic plant flowers, which he said should form a protective barrier to keep the vampire at bay. Was it the garlic flower that had been placed in the casket with the Queen?

"Go on, Quincey." Urged Holmes.

"The funeral party arrived. Then, the service was taken. Afterward, six guardsmen in bearskin hats and full uniforms remained to watch over the casket. We stayed hidden, close by, intending to observe the grounds overnight."

"You expected something?" I said.

"Or someone?" Holmes said.

"I'm convinced of a connection between what we went through in Chislehurst and the relationship between

Napoleon III and the Queen." Said Quincey.

"We can't be certain. However, an impressive chain of logic to your reasoning does appear."

"It all leads to Dracula. I hoped he would appear."

"You were hiding in readiness for a confrontation?"

"Yes, I remained out of view of the guard, in a central position between the church and the mausoleum. The time on my pocket watch showed nearly midnight when my attention was brought to the path closest to the mausoleum."

"He appeared?"

"No, it was a sound of steady and slow marching coming from the distance. The stamping and scraping of hard soles of military boots on the pathway grew louder as the group approached. The steps moved ever closer. Then, out of the mist, a parade became visible."

"You say a parade?"

"Yes, well, it's more of a military column. A coffin was in the center of the line, held on a cart. The casket was plain but the same size as that of the Queen's, but there was something different about it."

"The Queen then?"

""I cannot be certain the casket was white and had weight. Other than that, I could not say."

"Then what?"

"The column of men made its way from St. George's chapel, where I knew the coffin lay in state under military guard, towards the mausoleum."

"I observed the casket first taken into the mausoleum, then returned moments before the church chimes struck midnight.

"There was no indication of why the coffin was moved back and forth."

"Maybe to remove the remains before the planned burial two days later?" I said.

"I constructed a bivouac with fallen branches and leaves. We remained in hiding, keeping each other warm. A cold nose woke me awake on the morning, the day of the burial.

"Snow had started to fall, cover the ground, and assist in the camouflage. We remained still and bore the cold. We waited for the service. It was then I heard footsteps beside my hiding spot."

"You were discovered?" I asked.

"No, we stayed silent and hidden, with the merest of holes to observe through. There stood a figure covered in a black cloak and a dark cap.

"A figure in a black cloak, my word."

"The cloak had some sort of golden chain linked across its lapels. It furled upwards in the wind, and I caught a glimpse of the man's clothing. A blue tunic. The uniform of the Blue Jacket's regiment. His boots shuffled in the snow directly adjacent to my opening, obscuring my view of the mausoleum. I feared I would miss direct sight of the burial. On hearing the parade approach, the man started to mumble strange words before running. He disappeared into the woods."

"Holmes, I should say that the description of the man in the cloak has raised my attention."

"How so, Watson?"

"Just today, on my way here, I had an inkling I was being followed by a man dressed just as Quincey describes."

"You tested your assumption?"

"I was hurrying, but I did notice a golden object fixed in his hand."

"A ring?"

"It was too distant for me to be able to confirm the matter."

"Then, we should first try to locate this man and determine his objective."

Holmes faced the boy.

"Quincey, the soldier in the cloak, do you recall his words?"

"Mostly garbled mumbling. But a name was in there. Percy, yes, Percy Phony, or something like it, if I recall correctly."

"Percy Phony, eh? Never heard of the man. Sounds like a villain, eh?" I said.

"I'm confused. What bearing do these events have on our purpose here, Holmes? Our matter presses on the security of Europe!" said Bellinger.

"This cloaked man may be the link to your conspiracy that we seek." Holmes turned to Bellinger, then to Quincey, "your book of scraps."

"Yes sir," the boy ran to his room and returned with his well-kept book, filled with now yellowing newspaper cuttings.

"Visit the article which set us on our first case, 'Lifeblood,' as the good doctor names it."

Quincey placed the book on the table, and we gathered around the boy in a semi-circle and looked over his shoulder as he turned to a page close to its beginning. And there it was, a neatly cut, fading square of newspaper print: 'Ghost ship runs aground in Whitby.'

"What of this, Holmes? Do you see a connection?" I asked.

"The name of the ship Quincey?"

The boy ran his fingers through the print until it stopped mid-paragraph.

"It was called the Demeter, Mr. Holmes."

Holmes returned to his seat and gazed into the heath

and its flickering flames. The rest of us remained standing. We waited for Holmes to speak, but he remained fixed in his stare as though his brain was turning its cogs to a solution to the puzzle. Or, more likely, he had the solution and was considering its impact on us all.

"Holmes, what do you make of this?" Bellinger asked.

"The Eleusinian mysteries."

"Mysteries? I know nothing of such matters, Holmes. Again, I remain perplexed by this line of interest."

"The ancient Greek goddess, Demeter."

"Other than Demeter, the strange name of the so-called ghost ship, you have me baffled, Holmes."

"Greek mythology. Zeus took Demeter's daughter against her will to an underworld kingdom. Demeter searched for her daughter all around the world without success. In her distress and to coerce Zeus to allow the return of her daughter, she caused terrible suffering on the people."

"The delivery of Dracula to England," I said, receiving a nod of acknowledgment from Holmes.

"And you say what we have in our hands is nothing greater than a 'story' Holmes, huh!" said Chesterfield, Raising the book from his lap and waving the pages in frustration toward the great detective.

"The daughter's name was Persephone," Holmes said,

his face refusing to issue any sign of satisfaction. "You find the connection, Earl?"

"Percy Phony, Persephone! As whispered by the cloaked man!" Said Quincey.

9

PERSEPHONE

The room was again silent, save for the spluttering of the fire in the hearth. Bellinger's eyes turned to a blank stare, and his face dropped into a look of confusion. Beside him, the Earl brushed his palm back and forth over the face of the document as it lay on his lap, his lips pursed until they were nothing but drained lines.

"You say that a vessel christened Demeter first brought the terror to our shores, Holmes?" Asked Chesterfield.

"Of that, there is no doubt."

"And you infer that the name Persephone is connected to these current events?"

"The names connect, and that is of no coincidence. So, yes, that is my conjecture."

"Ridiculous!"

"My many investigations have, as a rule, shown that the more bizarre a thing is, the less mysterious it proves to be."

"Chesterfield, the ship. No one here could possibly know," Said Bellinger.

"Know what?" I asked.

"Early this year, there was an incident involving a schooner. Shipping out of Portsmouth. Its name was Alicia. The boat charted to carry unknown cargo to Calais, disappeared in a fog. The vessel and all hands were lost without a trace. No wreckage, no reported landing at other ports," Bellinger continued.

"I don't find the connection," I said.

"The manifest left at the port showed the boat to have been renamed Persephone on the outset of what was to be the final voyage."

"And there you have it," said Holmes, slowly drifting to the window and standing close to its edge. Bellinger and Chesterfield sat, becalmed on the settee.

"Watson, come to the window and examine the man standing in the doorway opposite without letting yourself be discovered."

I moved around the furniture, went to the window opening, and pressed my back to the wall. Leaning carefully to venture my eye around the edge of the frame, I searched for the man. There he was. A tall figure in a long dark overcoat and a hat covering his face.

"Why, that's the fellow I saw following me earlier! He's been shadowing us, which means he's likely involved in this mystery," I exclaimed.

"Quincey, exchange position with Dr. Watson, taking the same precaution and view the figure if you will," said Holmes.

"Sir, that is the man I saw at the burial!" Said Quincey. Prince grumbled, stirred from his dormant curl, and darted to his master's side.

"But about this case, Holmes?" asked Bellinger.

"It has been in progress for years, and I have been on it for that distance. Gentlemen, I will take this case. Our aim is to find Dracula and his followers. I believe the Count is in Europe, but we must take our leave and chase down this unknown figure for now."

Holmes struck out his hand, shook on the deal with Bellinger and the Earl, and made his way to the door. He turned.

"You are familiar with Inspector Lestrade at the Yard?"

"Why yes," replied Bellinger.

"Then we will report our findings through the telegraph directly to inspector Lestrade for your attention. Good day to you both, gentlemen."

"Watson, Quincey, follow me and make haste before this figure disappears again."

We took to our heels and followed in line astern behind Holmes. Knowing the temperature and the possibility of a chase, my jacket remained on its hook. Almost tumbling down the stairs, the detective was ahead by two strides as we exited the front door of 221B.

We all glanced across the street to where I had seen the shadow positioned. The same space was now occupied with nothing more than a swirl of litter, twisting around the cobbled street like a hungry seagull.

"He's gone!" said Quincey. We shifted our view up and down the street. Nothing but the bustle of a normal busy day. Hats are in every direction, and there is no distinction between the innocent and the wanted man.

"Bring the dog." Holmes turned to Quincey, who directed Prince to the spot where we had seen the figure only minutes before. The dog circled for a moment his snout picking up the air and savoring it as would the best taster of wine. His role in the investigation was crucial, and we all knew it.

"Find!" Quincey commanded. The dog understood. His frame tightened as he directed his snout towards the East.

"Hopefully, he hasn't taken a cab," I said.

"He wouldn't be the only one to decide against logic." Said Holmes, turning a glance in my direction. "Quick, pick up the pace, gentlemen."

Led by the dog, we followed the scent for a quarter mile, winding between streets through alleys and pathways. Our prey remained hidden from our sight. Then, amongst a line of waiting cabs, Prince stopped in his tracks and turned in a circle. The dog's nose was almost attached to his tail, indicating that the scent no longer led us.

"Prince has lost the scent!" cried Quincey, his voice filled with disappointment. It was a setback we hadn't anticipated and weighed heavily on us momentarily.

"He has escaped then," I said.

"I think I know his direction," said Holmes, "to a cab, and we might head him off."

"But where?" I spluttered as we entered the nearest waiting cab. Holmes gave the driver the destination. My heart leaped upon hearing the direction. I was filled then with a familiar dread and apprehension as we hurtled through the streets of London.

10

OLD GROUND

Our direction took us towards the river. The bustle of industrial machinery and clacking of steel chain filled the air. Between the smoke-stained stone faces of familiar buildings and through their simmering grey slate rooftops I caught sight of the first Tower. The menacing silhouette of the Bridge to which it belonged followed. Hairs on my flesh prickled as the dark memory of our first confrontation with Dracula swept like a tide across my mind. My skin rippled and bumped, shivers took the back of my hands and neck.

I pressed backwards into my seat and steadied my breath. Holmes and the dog hung their heads out of the side windows as the cab bounced on the cobbles. The first sign that we were closing in our pursuit was issued as a soft growl as Prince caught a familiar scent.

"Stop now, driver!" Holmes shouted.

We were thrown forward in our seats as the cab came to a rapid halt.

"Take care of the driver, Watson." The others leaped out of our carriage as I remained.

"That'll be a shilling." The driver said, his eager hand reached towards me. My fingers fumbled eagerly through several pockets as they searched then found the payment. I jumped into the street in chase and turned to the driver.

"Call Scotland Yard, ask for Lestrade and tell him Sherlock Holmes needs his assistance here." I instructed as I put the required coins into his hand.

"Sherlock Holmes, the detective?"

"Yes, my man, the detective, hurry on now."

The driver nodded and set off, hopefully to find the nearest constable or telephone. I had no confidence that my instructions would be acted upon.

Meantime, my companions had galloped fifteen yards ahead and were disappearing into the opening of the street door to Tower Bridge. By the time I entered they, led by the dog, were already climbing the stairway leading to the pedestrian passageway linking the two towers together. The same passageway where the grotesque had once gathered to serve their master.

"Stop there!' I heard Holmes cry, followed by the sound of a scuffle and Prince barking.

As I burst through the entrance I could see a wild confrontation in progress. The man in the cloak was standing against the struts which formed a barrier to the open air above the grey waters flowing more than one-hundred and thirty feet below. Prince had set himself in front of the man and was snarling between bared teeth.

I doubled over, resting my hands above my knees and took steadying deep breaths. Holmes turned for a moment and shook his head in my direction.

"Really, Watson."

We could all now clearly see the countenance which stood before us. A broad and tall figure, a dark cloak wrapped around his shoulders. Underneath a military uniform. There was something about it. A familiar style, but not one I recognized being of a British regiment. A dark blue material, horizontal embroidered rows of grey piping, probably formerly white, braid stretched across the front. The collar and cuffs a tattered dark red.

"He's a soldier!" I said.

"Give yourself up man, we only want to talk." Holmes said.

"I cannot, and will not!" the man, his voice seemingly emanating from a gravel filled bucket, growled back.

"Just tell us why you have been following us and we shall be on our way."

"You know why, Mr. Holmes. A great detective, aren't you? Ha, ha, ha. You know exactly why!" the man sneered, lowered his head in a bow, flapped his arms wide beath the cape and suddenly lurched forward like an eagle descending on his prey. At the same time his boot struck out at the dog, hitting the pup in the ribs with a dull crack.

Prince was thrown across the space, landing with a grunt as the hound's spine crashed against the passage wall, where he lay motionless. Holmes held between the man's arms grappled as he was turned towards the open stanchions, his hair twisted in the breeze.

"Prince!" Quincey shouted in horror and ran to the side of his dog in desperation, throwing his cane along the steel floor with a rattle. He bent beside the injured pup and stroked his hand against Prince's head.

"Watch out!" I cried as I leaped forward. I grabbed at the soldier's neck and shoulders from behind. There was no grip to be had. My hands slipped on the material and his flesh, both of which had a coating of wet, slimy grease.

As my fingers flailed against the cloth to get hold the soldier twisted. Then with a single grunt and quick movement, the man threw out his left arm to his rear, catching the side of my head with a hard blow. The percussion almost burst my eardrum, and I fell to the floor, almost unconscious.

I blinked against the light and watched helplessly as the violent scuffle took place in front of me. A dance the like of which I had seen before. When Dracula took Lord Godalming before our eyes in the Exeter theater.

The soldier's right hand kept Holmes by the neck, the boney fingers white with effort. The detective's feet lifted off the floor and reached unsuccessfully for a solid purchase.

"You have failed again, Mr. Holmes" grunted the soldier as he pressed his mouth close to the side of Holmes' neck.

From the corner of my eye, I caught a movement. It was Quincey, cane in hand. Quincey stepped forward with his stick lowered. I watched on as his training under Barton-Wright in the art of Bartitsu came to him like someone returning to a bicycle after years of abstinence.

There was little room in the passageway to swing the stick to its full extent, and even as my head swirled, I couldn't imagine any way that the boy could generate a force which would dissuade the attacker. Quincey assumed a sort of guard position. A similar stance one would see in a fencing match. His right foot extending towards the left side of the scuffle. The boy edged closer until he caught a glance from the soldier.

"Let him go!" Quincey shouted.

"Step away from this boy. I will deal with your fate when the time comes," the soldier grunted through gritted teeth.

Quincey threw out his cane towards the left cheek of his opponent's face, which drew the soldiers' left hand to defend against the strike. Quincey straightened to his full height and caught the man's left arm in his palm, pushing upward then pulling on the clothing to effect a change in balance.

Quincey then in the same movement, crouched as low as possible, thrusting his cane through the soldier's legs. A quick twist of the stick between the man's knees and then against his thighs exerting sufficient leverage to throw the soldier against the stanchions.

The fight had released Holmes from the wrestle and the detective quickly pushed the flat palms of both hands into the chest of the off-balance soldier, who continued to slip on his feet. The man whirled his arms in a desperate attempt to grab anything solid but couldn't prevent his upper body squeezing through the opening and pulling the rest to fall. Spinning like an autumn leaf from the bridge into the river below.

11

DREDGE

"Your message, Dr. Watson," a familiar voice came at me through the high-pitched ringing in my ear. "I received your message."

I turned away from the street-level parapet of the bridge. On my left, I found the welcome figure of Inspector Lestrade as he tipped his hat in my direction. His eyes, set in his familiar thin, ferret-like face, darted between me and towards the dirty, swirling river below.

"Excuse me, Inspector. My hearing is somewhat disturbed." I said, hardly hearing my own voice. I moved across Lestrade to stand with my, at present, somewhat better ear closest to the conversation.

Meanwhile, to our right, Holmes leaned over the parapet and scanned the water with a fierce intent for any sign of the soldier. The river flowed, curdling and weaving against itself. The dark boundary between air and below covered everything that lay beneath its surface with a blanket of silt and scum. Quincey slumped on the pavement. His arms wrapped around the dog as he cradled the limp pup on his lap. Prince had his eyes half-open and made disconcerting wines of discomfort.

"Tell me, what is the event, Dr?" Lestrade said. "After we received your message, with no indication of the purpose, I might add, we had many calls regarding a man falling or jumping from the walkway." Lestrade peered upward at the passage above. "The same event?"

"He was a man who had been following us. We noticed his presence in various locations over the last few weeks. A soldier, by all appearances. In a somewhat unfamiliar uniform. To my eyes anyway." I said.

"He jumped in suicide, then?"

"No, there was a struggle between us beforehand."

"You threw him off the bridge?"

"I had sufficient reason, Inspector."

"A consistent response from those accused of such offenses."

I gestured towards Quincey and Prince, then pointed into the wake of muddy water flowing beneath our position.

"Inspector, as you can see, the man hurt the dog and blew out my eardrum before the boy here aided in depositing the villain in the river."

"I see. Then the boy's hand threw him overboard?" Lestrade said.

"Well, his cane did," I replied.

A look of confusion passed across the sharp contours of the Inspector's face. The narrowing eyes betrayed the fact that he really didn't.

"I'll get some of my men to drag the river, but the body has likely washed downstream with the tide, and it won't be discovered for a week until it works its way to the surface through bloating."

Holmes approached. The few pedestrians who had seen the man's fall became less interested and began to leave the scene to continue their day. Lestrade acknowledged Holmes.

"Mr. Holmes. Perhaps you can shed more light on the situation for me?"

"Inspector, I'm sure Watson has provided a suitable outline. We followed the man who had been, in turn, following us. As we confronted him, he attacked us. Then, through the struggle and not due to our desire, he fell to his death. However, there is more to this encounter."

"Tell me, Holmes," Lestrade said.

"The man informed us that he had been instructed to follow us. In effect, a messenger sent to alert us of his master's intent.

"Messenger, eh? Rather more than that, don't you think, Holmes?" I said.

"The man's reaction and fight were a consequence of being cornered, nothing more, Watson."

"As you say, Holmes, but his intent was to kill us all!"

"If his mission was to do that, then he undoubtedly would have before now. He had many opportunities. Quincey at the Queen's burial, you in the street today, and all of us a moment ago."

"But for the boy, he would have!"

"I'm certain a report of our movements and meetings was his only task here."

Perched elbow to elbow, we continued to lean over the parapet and gaze into the water. Now and then, sparks of daylight reflected from the river's surface, bringing images of ghostly faces to my imagination.

"Then who is his master, Holmes?" Lestrade asked.

"I have no alternative to believe that we are about to engage again with our greatest and most cunning enemy."

"Dracula!" I said. My head throbbed as I spoke the name.

Lestrade stumbled backward, his face aghast. We remained silent as his men arrived at the bridge and started throwing grappling hooks into the water for nearly two hours.

The mud plumes that rose against the river's surface like swirling thunderclouds did not dull their effort. The constables had pulled various items of discarded detritus from the dark water. The hooks pulled old shoes, baby carriage wheels, steel rails, and other objects without purpose from where they had meant to rest. These items were piled unceremoniously against the bridge wall like a museum exhibit. Then there was a cry.

"Over here, sir," a policeman shouted. Two of his colleagues rushed beside him. The three worked together, pulling on the rope in a steady but powerful rhythm. Lestrade, Holmes, and I ran towards the activity.

Gradually, from the water, appeared a tangled clump of clothing spinning on the end of a tri-pronged grappling hook. A cape, sodden with water, draped around what appeared to be a body like a cocoon. As the object swam around, a gap in the cape revealed flashes of blue. It was the soldier's jacket, flapping open as the remains turned in the air.

"Pull it up!" shouted Lestrade.

With half a dozen coordinated heaves, the body was deposited over the parapet onto the pavement with a soggy thud. As the form spread on to the ground, a bony hand slapped onto the cobbled street. The cape opened and confirmed the blue jacket and, for the first time that I had noticed, dirty dark red trousers.

"The body is already decayed!" I shouted in surprise. The flesh of the hand is thin and transparent. The bones are held together by withered yellow tendons. The face of the man is more than lifeless. I likened it to the ghastly features of the young victims we had viewed at Chislehurst. Only in this instance did the underlying age of the corpse advance by many years.

"Then it cannot be the same as we seek, Dr. How could it be?" said Lestrade.

"It must be. It wears the same clothing and cape," I answered.

Holmes settled on his hunches and reached for the limp mass of the hand, turning the sack of bones. The wrist cracked as the knuckles faced upwards, and the fingers spread like a dead crab.

"It is the same, Inspector, see."

On the third finger, a gold ring sparkled in the sun. At the same time, Holmes reached into his jacket pocket and took out a similar object. It was the ring we had recovered from amongst the rubble within the Chislehurst Caves. He set them side by side. The rings were identical and bore the same inscription: 'OCCULTA SANGUINE.'

"Evidence from our encounter at Chislehurst, Inspector."

"I say, Holmes," I gasped.

"Then, you have in mind the criminal Dracula, Holmes?" Lestrade said, his complexion turned a sallow grey as he rocked backward, steadying himself against the cold stone of the bridge's parapet.

"Yes, the entity behind this, Inspector. I would suggest that anyone wandering with such a piece be judged part of the scheme. Your men must be advised to express caution should they encounter associates of the Count. There is no doubt that there is a wider plan afoot," Holmes said, then turned towards me.

"Watson, I think you will find that the soldier's uniform is that of the French Imperial Guard of Napoleon III. A highly decorated dark blue tunic, red collar, cuffs and trousers."

"But what is the meaning?" I said.

Holmes pulled a length of cape away from the body and played his index finger through a hole that followed a path through the back, then front, of the blue tunic uniform. Holmes glanced at me questioningly and wiggled his finger like a worm on a hook. It was at that point that I realized.

"The diameter of a musket shot!" I said.

"Your deductive skills are evidently intact, Watson."

"Montparnasse cemetery in Paris!" shouted Quincey. "I recall the report. Imperial guards were stationed to protect the area from 'vampires.' Something was spotted and then shot at as it climbed a high wall. At least one of the bullets wounded it, but the target escaped. The next day, investigators recovered tatters of blue fabric from the scene. Could that be the same blue fabric, Mr. Holmes?"

"And so are yours, my boy. So are yours." Holmes whispered to himself.

12

CLOUDS

We hailed a cab to return to 221B. We spent the journey huddled in silence, apart from my ear, which continued to ring in my head like an untuned church bell, a constant reminder of the danger we had just escaped. Beside me, Quincey wrapped the pup in his jacket and held him tightly on his lap as we bounced through the streets. Now and then, the dog whimpered softly.

Holmes remained deep in thought, his eyebrows pinched upwards over his nose. Lestrade would join us after he had cleared the scene at the Bridge. Mrs. Hudson greeted us as we entered the building and, seeing the limping dog, immediately started to fuss about him.

"Oh my, my poor boy," the housekeeper poured herself on the dog, engulfing the hound in her arms. Let me get you some food. The dog licked her face and wagged his tail enthusiastically.

"A sudden recovery, eh?" I said.

"I'm sure that you're quite capable of taking care of yourselves, Dr." Mrs. Hudson huffed as she guided the dog into the kitchen. "I'll bring up some tea once I tend to this poor mite. A good bowl of stew will see you, right, eh, boy?"

"Come, we must focus on the matter at hand," Holmes said as he ascended the stairs.

The morning exercise caused such an ache in my legs as we chased Holmes into the lounge. There was a cold, empty air about the place. The conversation with Bellinger and Chesterfield seemed like an age ago. They had left and taken their book with them. The fire in the room was now nothing more than embers, pulsing steadily in the morning light. I considered filling the hearth with new coal, then thought more about it. The temperature of the day and the heat generated through our own activities called for the ashes to remain so cool for the time being.

Holmes hunched in his chair, preparing his pipe for the usual ritual. I positioned myself as usual in my seat, directly opposite his seat. Thankfully, the ringing in my ear had now subsided to a low hum. Prince wandered through the doorway and made his way slowly but purposefully to the front of the heath. The dog circled and wearily plopped himself onto the rug. The dog's health was greatly improved, aided by a good helping of Mrs. Hudson's beef stew. Quincey ruffled the dog's coat and then sat at the table, pacing through the pages of the day's newspapers. He always sought articles of particular interest to be snipped for his collection.

"What's to be done, Holmes', I asked.

Holmes lit his pipe and puffed out several slow breaths before answering.

"First, the boy must return to his barracks before he gets too much trouble."

"But, Mr. Holmes!" Quincey protested.

"Holmes is correct, Quincey, and you know it. There will be discipline and likely confinement to your academy due to your absence. This is not a matter to be taken lightly," I added, trying to impress upon Quincey the gravity of his situation.

"But you see how we can help." Quincey protested.

"A better help is to have you here," said Holmes.

"You are traveling away?" asked Quincey.

"Yes, Watson and I must depart for Europe and Budapest as soon as possible, by tonight's train, if the schedule permits. This trip is of utmost importance," Holmes declared.

"Budapest?" I said.

"Recall our conversation with Bellinger and Chesterfield and the possible connection with the

Ancient Mysteries and Budapest?"

"Persephone?" Quincey chimed from his seat at the table.

"Yes, in particular, the Eleusinian Mysteries. The rites that are remarked to stem from ancient Greece and Rome. These are times well before the Christian era. Times marked by dark beliefs and religions corrupted by some for their own purpose. Also, recognize that these historical rites bear a very striking resemblance in many points to elements of the rituals of Freemasonry."

"Freemasonry Holmes? A society marked for good and through many deeds set about doing such good for society?"

"That may be the case for the organization in general and the belief of many of its members. I want to remind you of the discoveries of our investigation, which you named 'Imperial' Watson. Do you recall Pike's prediction of world wars? And how Freemasonry is to be corrupted to manufacture the circumstances leading to the first great war."

"Vaguely Homes. You think Dracula is using his dark forces as an agency to gather storm clouds around the ones seeking to implement the forecast Bellinger and Chesterfield brought to this very room?"

"Indeed, Watson, and the reason that we need to venture to Budapest, for that city, is the location predicted to become the focal point for this effort. I know two groups recently merged, the Blue Lodge and the Scottish Rite, to form the Symbolic Grand Lodge of Hungary in Budapest. I believe this organization may be the vehicle used for Dracula's corruption, even though they may not realize the fact."

"Pike's idea would play into Dracula's hands. A Satanic Order, Watson. A corruption of the Scottish Rite. Within our investigations at Chislehurst, we found connections to France, Scotland, and perhaps our dear cousins in the United States. I'm convinced more than ever that the idea invades all major capitals and persuades political power."

"Paris Holmes! I recall the flower in the painting in the Impy, the Lotus!" I said eagerly.

"Quite Watson. The Rite and its members are set to become the foundation that brings this Luciferian conspiracy to its final stage. Pike has written that this effort might take one hundred years or more to establish members of the Rite as leaders of the entire world. At such a time, they will impose a totalitarian dictatorship upon those who remain. A timeframe that is inconsequential to one such as Dracula."

Holmes rose from his chair. He circled the room, his teeth clamped on the pipe as it spewed foul smoke spluttering around the room.

"Then think Watson of the connections we have discovered which could enable this, between Paris, London, and now Budapest. Think of the tensions which run through the Balkans at this very moment. Bellinger and Chesterfield spoke of it. We are on the periphery of the plot intended to manufacture a world war."

"Budapest. It is close to Dracula's original home, is it not?" Quincey asked.

"That may be the case, my boy, but it shall make no difference to our task, and you must return to your barracks with the utmost speed."

"What if you need us, Mr. Holmes?" Quincey gestured to Prince.

"You need rest. Your ability is of greater need here. We shall be traveling on the Orient Express from Paris to Budapest. I shall contact you by telegraph as we stop at various cities if the need arises. Continue with your daily examination of the press. Relay any information you might discover from whatever source you sense is connected. Keep in contact with Bellinger and Chesterfield. Do you understand?"

"Yes, sir," Quincey called the dog to his side. I hailed a cab to take them back to the barracks and then returned to Holmes.

"Watson, we'll require night train passage from Folkestone to Boulogne, then onto Paris to board the Orient Express to take us to Budapest. Also, send this telegraph." Holmes scribbled a note and handed it to me. It was addressed to Laskaris, The Red Frog, Kristina, First District, Budapest. The remainder was in French, which I could not decipher.

'DEUX JOURS JUSQU'À NOTRE FIANÇAILLES.'

"We have both business which has been done and business to do," Holmes said.

13

NIGHT TRAIN

I collected the tickets for our journey from the nearest Peninsular and Oriental company broker and set them neatly on the table. The night train ran from Charing Cross Station and would depart at 4:30 p.m. that evening. We would need to be there at 4 p.m. at the latest to load whatever baggage we would take. The trip to Budapest from Paris would take us two days.

Holmes had also directed that I telegram the Municipal Council of Paris for an appointment to visit the catacombs the next day in the early afternoon. The purpose of the visit was still to be revealed. However, I suspected that it was linked to our discoveries at Chislehurst. Even so, the thought of wandering around a damp cavern lined with human skulls and bones did not fill me with excitement.

It was just after 1 p.m. when Mrs. Hudson ushered Lestrade into 221B. The Inspector appeared in the doorway. The ashen residue of the morning's events remained embedded upon his face. His gaze was drawn and weary as he fixed his attention upon Holmes. Lestrade began to speak; there was an urgency in his voice.

"Mr. Holmes, you need to explain what on earth is going on here. I trust we do not have the beginnings of a repeat of events from those years ago. I cannot, for the life of me, wander through such a dark conflict again without preparation."

"Your suspicion may be correct, for I fear we have all witnessed the start of another chapter. One which will not, this time, be played out on the streets of London."

"The earlier event, which I shall call it that because I still do not know its reason, requires explanation. It appears to be suicide, but you say not. The body, or should I say remains, is aged longer than the timeline you describe. But didn't this death happen on these very streets?"

"The event you attended was a consequence of plans already in place, Inspector. Plans which are fixed to cumulate in Europe. You have witnessed remains of the like before, have you not?"

"Well, yes, I concede that I have. Remarkably only in your presence, Holmes. It still remains a shock."

"Take a seat and calm yourself," I said. Lestrade took a seat on the settee.

"You say Europe, Holmes?" Lestrade said before

standing again and fidgeting towards the table.

"Budapest, to be precise." Replied Holmes.

Lestrade glanced down at the table and reached out to fan the travel tickets apart like a deck of playing cards. The small rectangles of paper shuffled at the end of his long, thin fingers. He leaned closer to read from them, passing his eyes over the itinerary.

"Charing Cross to Folkestone, a crossing of the English Channel to Boulogne, a train from Boulogne to Paris, then a train from Paris to Budapest. Hmm, the Orient Express. No expense spared!"

"The fastest and most efficient route to our destination, Inspector. We only have a limited opportunity to prevent a world disaster."

"It will still take some four days from now," I said.

"A world disaster?" said Lestrade, his features gaining an almost impossible sharpness as he ran an index finger to cup his unshaven chin. "If there is evidence of an impending event of such widespread impact, then wouldn't the powers of Europe be best advised to be ready? And for that matter, wouldn't political motions already be in place?"

"You know yourself of Lord Bellinger?"

"The ex-prime minister? Of course."

"He was here today with Earl Chesterfield. I had

doubts myself until today's encounter."

"Doubts, Holmes?"

"I struggled to accept the forecast laid before me. Bellinger and Chesterfield provided privileged information regarding matters of national importance. Information which I cannot divulge. Suffice it to say, the great European nations are already infiltrated. Subverted, eager to embark on an opportunity to rule the continent. Each country believes that they are the rightful masters. But now we know the likely mastermind and his resources."

Lestrade nodded and played the ornate ticket for the Orient Express between his fingers.

"I see. You think by deduction that Budapest is where your advisory hides?"

"He does not hide Lestrade. He signals his position like a feint of a general. Arranging his forces and luring us into his trap."

"Yet you follow his direction easily."

"He knows I know, and I know that he does."

"A sort of riddle then."

"Only to some, Inspector. In the meantime, I require you to contact Bellinger or Earl Chesterfield; as I say, they both have this knowledge. You must relay to them today's happenings and that we are embarking to Budapest this very evening. We will be open to contact via telegraph as we pass through the various cities. Do not hesitate to do so."

"But such messages are easy to intercept, Holmes."

"That is the very purpose, Lestrade."

14

CROSSING

After booking and processing our luggage with the labels provided, the ticket master called the porter to take our boxes and cases to the baggage car. At the same time, I ensured that our tickets and receipts were tucked securely into the inside pocket of my jacket. Our packing accounted for the dress etiquette required for our journey aboard the express, so our cases numbered four.

"We will need those two small cases delivered to our cabins on the express; the remainder may be stored in the baggage car," I told the well-rounded porter. His breeches lifted above his ankle, revealing bright red socks and scuffed brown leather shoes.

"I shall note that on your labels. It will be taken care of, sir; further instruction will not be needed." He said as a matter of fact.

We boarded the train at Charing Cross and started our overnight journey to Paris. The carriage was full of workers returning home from London and others perhaps journeying to Folkestone, but no further. An unknown number would be taking the same path as us.

"Keep your eyes open and your wits about you, Watson," said Holmes.

"You think we are followed?"

"I don't think I know. Observe the woman in the dark overcoat and deep-brimmed hat. She's not just a random passenger, Watson. She's a key player in this mystery," Holmes said, his eyes narrowing with determination.

"I see her," I replied.

The woman, small in stature, was located seven rows in front of our seats on the opposite side of the carriage. Her orientation faced our direction, but from what I could observe, she did not study at us at all. I noted that the woman maintained the same distant stare sideways out of the window, even when the carriage passed through tunnels, and there was nothing for her to see but the smoke-stained brickwork as it flashed by.

"She doesn't look in our direction, Holmes. Her head turned, fixed outside the carriage at every moment. In any case, the brim of her hat hides the direction of her eyes."

"The reflection, Watson, observe at the next tunnel."

I waited for the next tunnel, and then, as I felt the air

pressure change and the echo of the engine reverberate, daylight disappeared. The darkness outside and the brightness of the cabin's interior lights turned the window into a mirror. The reflection of the woman's face became suddenly more apparent, and under the brim of her hat, I could clearly see the glint of her eyes in the glass.

"I can observe her face, Holmes, and her eyes."

"Then she can see yours as well."

"She is a follower of the Count?"

"Not the only one."

"You have me a nervous wreck, Holmes."

"The better to keep you at your most alert."

We reached Folkestone. Holmes grabbed onto my elbow.

"Wait, allow the others to disembark," Holmes said.

The passengers, including the woman, crowded the platform, and we soon lost sight of our target. Her small stature swallowed within the mingled bustle of bodies. The transfer to the steam packet ship was quickly done as the train stopped directly at the dockside. I continued to search, looking up and down the dockside and the boarding ramp to the boat, but the woman was nowhere in sight. Only eleven others headed from the train, following our direction.

I counted them carefully: seven men, three women,

and a baby in a small carriage. Two of the women, one dressed almost entirely in white, and the child traveled together. Of the men, one stood taller than the others and wore a distinctive hat, making his stature even greater. Another, wearing a tweed jacket, carried a wooden box under his arm and an unusually shaped case by his side.

We headed directly to our transport, the South-Eastern packet ferry S.S. Dutchess of York. The dock transfer was bustling with activity as porters manhandled the luggage from the baggage car to the ship's hold. I hauled myself up the gangplank and stepped onto the clean deck, keeping a downward eye so as not to lose my footing. As soon as I raised my head, a blustery, salty breeze slapped me directly into the face. There was no mistaking the musky and mysterious smell of the sea that accompanied our departure.

The crew lined up to greet us and direct us to our cabins and the lounge. The first-class saloon was well-furnished with plush, upholstered leather seating. Large windows offered views of the sea.

"I'm hoping that the journey is smooth, Holmes," I said, knowing that seasickness was a frequent companion for many travelers. I hoped that I would not be joining the many pale faces and uneasy stomachs already milling about the saloon.

"Time for a brandy, Watson."

My stomach twitched as I recalled Clements, the innkeeper at the Impy, who often would partake in a morning glass to calm his nerves.

"I think I'll stick with the ginger," I said, taking a small, wrapped hard sweet from my pocket. "I have found it to be a capital way to ease stomach worries." Holmes smiled slightly, then made his way to the lounge bar.

A loud clunk vibrated through the ship as the gear was engaged. Then, a steady increase in the engine's speed got us underway. The rhythmic thrum of the pistons and the chimney's release of steam set the soundtrack for our journey. In a matter of minutes, we left Folkestone Harbour's calm and entered the English Channel's choppy waters.

It was then I observed the tall man I had seen departing the train at Folkestone. I am determined to introduce myself as discretely as possible. He was standing against one of the large windows and conversing with a smaller gentleman. They were both staring at the open, swirling sea of the English Channel. I moved to be close enough to their position in order to better hear their conversation.

"I hear the crossing will be rough," said the smaller man.

"It appears like you may be right," replied his companion.

"Not for me. I have experienced far worse," the tall man replied. A large swell lifted the boat and dropped it at a faster rate. The smaller man's eyes rolled around like marbles.

"You make this journey often?"

"Yes, at least twice a month. It's work. the tall man replied.

"For your work?"

"Yes, in Budapest. I'm an importer of wines and other liquors."

"Any brandy? I hear it's perfect for staving off sickness. It's my first time crossing," I interjected.

"Unfortunately, my business is mainly fine wines, but I'm always on the lookout." The tall man replied.

"By the way, I'm John, John Watson. Nice to meet you both," I said, raising my hand to introduce myself.

"Garant Guinness," he replied.

"Henry Green," the smaller man said, keeping an involvement in the conversation, which was, for him, now only a by-product of the rolling boat. "It's my first time, as well." The package ship gave a giant undulating lurch and sent the blood from Green's face straight to his boots. I thought he might faint, so I gave him some encouragement in that direction.

"There's food at the bar, pickled eels, and the like," I said.

With that, Green pulled out a handkerchief and pushed it against his pale, thin lips with the flat of his open palm. The boat heaved upward, reached a peak, balanced momentarily, and then dropped like an anchor. Our stomachs were abandoned to find their own place as our guts revolved with the motion. Green's complexion lost any of the color it had retained, his skin turning to a creamy wax pallor. He waved his free hand like a flamenco dancer and exited the lounge to hang over the handrail on deck.

"Poor fellow, rather delicate, I fear," I said to Guinness.

"Hmm, he'll get his legs by the end of the trip, no doubt."

"You have no such weakness, I see."

"As I mentioned to Green, I'm an old hand at this. It's my business."

"All over Europe?"

"Presently Austria-Hungary, and more recently Budapest. I work as an import manager for fine wines. Hedges & Butler of London, Regent Street, you may have heard of us?"

"Probably too fancy for my taste, but Budapest, eh? That's a coincidence. My destination as well."

"I must say that your name does ring a bell, Mr. Watson. In what line of work are you engaged?"

"You could say..."

At that point, Holmes appeared at my shoulder.

"Watson, my dear fellow, apologies for the

interruption, but we must discuss our trip in our cabin."

With that, he pulled my shoulder to turn away from Guinness. And I excused myself with unease from his company.

"Holmes, that interruption was rather uncouth, don't you think?"

"You know the man?"

"Why yes, his name is Guinness, and he's an importer of wines..."

"Today," Holmes said, "we must keep our business as much to ourselves as we are able. Remember, there are other agencies afoot."

We turned into our cabin, and I slept for the remainder of the crossing. My days on the troop ships to India and the many ginger lozenges had prepared me well.

We woke up the following day and partook of breakfast in the lounge. I spotted Green as he meandered to a table, then left before his seat touched the chair to take up his position, bent over the handrail. On the bow, the bustling French port of Boulogne came into view.

We disembarked and waited at the railway station for the train. It was early morning when we stepped onto the train to begin our leg trip to Paris. There was no sign of Guinness or his hat.

15

PARIS

We arrived at Gare du Nord in Paris, slightly behind schedule, at 11:20 a.m. Our luggage would be transferred directly to the Gare de l'Est and loaded onto the train, ready for departure later that evening. Most passengers made their way to the nearest hotel. We had business to attend to and hurried out of the station.

The street outside the station bustled with activity. The pavement was lined with food carts of various types. I had read of these so-called 'harlequin' merchants, who sold leftover food they had collected from wealthy Parisian houses to the throngs of hungry travelers.

"They're renowned for offering good quality food, Holmes," I said, my stomach rumbling in anticipation. Holmes didn't respond.

My appetite engaged with the aroma of various cooking as it floated through the air. The poultry, fish, oysters, and roast beef meals smelled delicious, but Holmes sprinted on without a second thought; even so, each vendor vied for our business as we passed at speed. I glanced back helplessly as meals were served to the throngs gathered beside the carts. The food, accompanied on a single plate with various side dishes and desserts, looked too good to pass, but we did.

"What time do we join the Express, Watson?"

"Hopefully, after we have eaten. The train departs at 7:50 p.m."

"Time enough to make a call at Montparnasse and then to explore the Catacombs, all before lunch."

"As you say, Holmes. You have a purpose in mind, I presume?"

"For you to remain observant, Watson, that's all I will ask of you today," he said, twisting his way through the crowd.

"As you say, Holmes."

Then we caught the natural smell of Paris, fresher than I had anticipated and feared. It was of great relief that the 'great stink' of recent years had been successfully dealt with. While I considered my observation, my mind wandered. In my absence of presence, I was almost run over by a fast-moving, well-fed porter pulling a large cart of crates behind him.

"Watch out. You almost took my foot off," I cried after the man as he ran by, leaving a flash of red at his ankles.

The porter turned and fixed me with a mixture of grimace and a smile. Then he pulled at the peak of his cap, which drew down to his eyebrows. I took this to be an apology and carried on in pursuit of Holmes.

After gathering some heat on my face from the midday sun, we set off. We hailed a fiacre, a narrow horse-drawn coach. The contraptions were all over the place.

"Bonjour, Cimetière du Montparnasse s'il vous plaît. » Holmes directed the driver.

"You speak French, Holmes."

"Through a tenuous relationship, Watson, but not well enough for us to be treated like locals."

Paris was complete with activity as the driver urged the horse onward and into the chaos that was the beautiful city. It was then, as I sat in the carriage, that I could observe the most magnificent buildings and architecture. We were traveling on the Boulevard de Magenta, a broad, tree-lined street framed on each side by tall stone façades of buildings dotted with wrought-iron balconies and capped with unusually shaped roofs.

As we sped by, the daily theater of Parisian life unfolded on the sidewalks. Café tables spilled onto the pavement, already occupied by the eager chatter of local gossip. Shops were filled with luxury goods and pastries.

"The exhibition tower, Holmes." I pointed in excitement as I glimpsed a view of the newly constructed Eiffel World Expo piece.

As we approached Montparnasse, the streets transitioned into a quiet residential neighborhood. Then I noticed the high protective stone walls that had allegedly failed to keep the vampire at bay. We had arrived at the cemetery's main gates; twenty-five minutes later, we had hailed the fiacre.

"L'emplacement du gardien du cimetières'il vous plaît?" asked Holmes, seeking direction from the driver as to the location of the cemetery caretaker, who he thought may be the best authority on the history of the vampire incidents.

A quick finger pointed through the entrance in the direction of a tall stone building that stood in the heart of a peaceful, green expanse of tree-lined pathways and grand stone and marble tombs. "Moulin de la Charité," came the reply.

Holmes led the way, and we passed through the gateway at speed. I opened my palm and ran my flat hand across the surface of the neatly finished powdery limestone blocks forming the tall walls surrounding the cemetery. Recessed between each row of stone were thin mortar joints. The lines were narrow, and I considered their gap was without sufficient articulation to allow a finger to purchase a hold.

"These walls, Holmes, I don't see how they could be

climbed without assistance."

"Everything is possible, Watson, until proven otherwise. Before we spend any time on that matter, let us attempt to locate a person who may know of the incident."

Close to the stone building, which, for all intents and purposes, appeared to be the bladeless body of a windmill, I glanced at the man. A small man, made smaller by a hunch in his spine, it was 'le gardien'.

Holmes approached and attempted to communicate with his knowledge of French. Fortunately, the guardian spoke passable English, and I was able to report the conversation as it happened without too much interpretation.

"You are 'le gardien' here?"

"Oui monsieur."

"I am Sherlock Holmes, the detective from London, and this is my assistant, Dr. Watson."

"I have heard of such a man called 'Holmes' in the newspapers. But why should you visit here?"

"I'm looking for some help. We are seeking anyone who may recall the story about the man who was said to have desecrated several graves in the cemetery some years ago. Do you know of the story?"

"Ah, oui, you must mean 'le vampire.' He was here, monsieur. We all know of the story. It is no dream; it is the facts that I have no doubt about."

"Why do you say that?"

"My family has worked in this place since before Napoleon III. You see, it is in our blood. My grandfather used to tell us the story, especially when we were in trouble. He used it as a warning. I remember the first time I heard it.

"It was one night, after my sister and I had been discovered climbing the trees in the cimetière, one of the branches of an old oak; you can still see it over there." The guardian stretched out his hand and jabbed a soil-stained finger in the general direction of a line of mature trees, then continued his explanation.

"I climbed too far. My sister shouted at me to stop, but I ignored her, as usual. Then, of course, the limb broke, and I fell onto a memorial stone. He slapped his hands together in a clap and smiled. You see, no one would have discovered, but I hurt my head, and my sister ran immediately for help." The guardian removed his cap and rubbed the back of his head wearily with the palm of his hand.

"The story?" asked Holmes.

"My grandfather was angry that our intrusion disturbed the dead. He threatened us that if we did not behave, then the authorities would come and take us to the catacombes. The place where living victims of the vampire were kept. My sister was very afraid and never came back into the cimetière. But, as you can see, the story did not stop me." a slight grin touched the edge of his lips.

"You didn't believe it?"

"No, no. I believe it. You see, the authorities did not tell the people the whole picture. Many citizens and witnesses to the events were paid to become silent. My grandfather was one."

"Did your grandfather inform you why the Emperor did this?"

"Oui monsieur, he told me that the Emperor directed the silence to halt the rumors and, as you would say, to protect the living from knowing of the event."

"Silence for what event?"

"The dead being taken as living."

"You mean the dead were living?"

"Oui, men raised from the grave taken to les catacombes. It was every night after the vampire had visited. Five, sometimes ten, were found awake but still lying in their graves. Almost thirty in all before the visits of the vampire ended. They were all men who had died in war, the soldiers of the empire. And that was only of this cimetière."

"There were others?"

"Many in Paris and its outskirts, I recall. That's the story as I know it. Les catacombes hold them still. Napoleon III ordered it so. They wait until called."

16

LES CATACOMBES

The time was almost 1 p.m. when we rejoined the fiacre and its driver where we had left them at the gates to the cemetery. The horse twitched nervously and moved the carriage back and forth as we climbed aboard. It reacted as though it was aware that a predator was stalking it and, therefore, us.

"Napoleon III, Holmes?"

"A connection which I suspected, Watson. We are getting deeper into this mystery and the picture is gaining clarity. We found a mention of the catacombes through our investigations at Chislehurst, did we not. This confirmation, albeit third hand, adds coal to the fire. The ends of the rope which attaches to Napoleon III become a tighter knot."

"I can't quite pull it together, Holmes. Victims of the

vampire transferred for storage. For what purpose?"

"Our next move will help bind the threads."

"There is unease all about. I feel eyes upon us." I said and reached beneath my jacket to grip the token that Van Helsing had presented to me all those years ago.

"Yes, Watson, do not be caught unawares. They are with us at all times."

"Et maintenant chauffeur on va aux catacombes," Holmes directed the driver, who without a word and a clip of the reigns released the relieved horse from its station. The entrance to the catacombs was within a very short distance from the cemetery in the Place d'Enfer.

"We could have easily walked, Holmes." I said.

"We'll require transportation to the railway station after our visit, Watson, so we will need to keep this carriage. Now, think back to Chislehurst. What do you recall of the Paris catacombes, Watson?" Holmes said as we traveled the three minutes to our destination. I massaged my chin with the forefinger and thumb of my right hand before answering.

"I think they are at least two-hundred years old, Holmes."

"Is that all you have?" Holmes raised his right eyebrow. "Any person on the streets of Paris would provide as much. Think on my good man. I know you have it."

Such a statement from the great detective meant that he did 'have it'. I concentrated and rubbed my chin like it was a magic lantern. I was seeking the release of a genie to carry the answer I needed. Then it came to me.

"Ahh! there is another connection, Holmes. A link to Montparnasse and what we just learned there. Around the same time as the reports of the vampire, Napoleon III descended into the catacombs with the Prince Imperial."

"There, you do have it!"

"What would they be doing down there?"

"That shall soon be discovered."

We left the carriage outside the entrance to the catacombs. Holmes turned and pressed a coin into the driver's shaking palm, then requested he wait for our return. The driver spoke quietly and with a quiver in his voice.

"J'attendrai votre retour comme vous le demandez, mais soyez prudent dans les profondeurs, monsieur. L'obscurité abrite les ombres vivantes de la mort. Le mal suit sans retenue ni regret."

"What did he say, Holmes?"

"He will wait for us. That is all you need to know." I found later what the translation of part of this meant, 'Darkness harbors the living shadows of death. Evil follows without restraint or regret.'

There was an attendant at the entrance, an official looking dark-haired man wearing a type of uniform and a small blue cap. The roundness of his face was exacerbated by a mustache that held his mouth tight against his nose. He welcomed Holmes on his approach.

"Monsieur Holmes, je suis informé de votre visite, bienvenue dans les catacombes."

His thick black mustache rippled. At the same time, he raised a hand, and its index finger wagged in front of our faces as he warned us to remain on the marked pathway. A stern warning of the more than one-hundred miles of tunnels beneath the vibrant streets of Paris was delivered. Any departure from the designated path could lead us to injury, or worse.

The attendant stepped to one side and gestured for us to enter. The doorway opened into a room which contained in its center a circular hole in the floor. A spiral staircase wound down into the depths of the catacombes. A hairy arm, complete with a simple tattoo etched on the forearm, extended from the attendant's cuff and removed a lantern from the wall. The man lit it and handed the light to Holmes.

Leaning over the banister, I peered into the abyss of the winding curl of the staircase, recalling with a shiver an image from our encounter with Dracula at Tower Bridge. The time we descended into the machine room to find the remains of Mina and

Jonathan.

"You don't think that he's down there, do you, Holmes?"

"If he is, then we'll both get a shock that we won't forget, won't we, my good man? Come, we have well over one hundred steps to descend. I have my revolver with me." Holmes tapped the side of his jacket.

As I planted my boot onto the first step, the whole world seemed to darken, as if the atmosphere had been alerted to recognize our arrival. I glanced back at the attendant. His moustache seemed to be sneering at our adventure. Did he know something that we didn't?

The deeper we travelled, the greater the feeling of suffocation as the air became more humid and the temperature colder. We reached the bottom of the staircase and paused, allowing our eyes to adjust to the flickering light thrown onto the walls of a precisely carved tunnel. It resembled the construction of a Victorian sewer, although I knew it was of a far greater age.

I followed as Holmes set off towards the ossuary. Then the architecture shifted, no longer resembling the Parisian sewers, but something far more ancient. After a distance, which felt longer than it was, we found a doorway. Above the opening, carved deep in its heavy stone lintel, were the words 'Arrête, voici l'empire de la mort.'

"What is its meaning, Holmes?"

"Stop, here is the empire of death."

"Very reassuring."

Holmes, holding the lantern at shoulder level with an outstretched arm, scanned through the narrow entry to the catacombs. His eyes flickered in time to the flame. I let out a nervous breath as we stepped through the doorway. Long, trembling shadows moved along the damp stone walls as we made our way forward.

I was as close behind Holmes as I could. Our footsteps crunched on the gravel as we walked. Sounds of our progress echoed throughout the passageways. Holmes halted in his tracks as the light of the lantern held the construction of the walls ahead in clear relief. Now I saw that this was truly a labyrinth of death. The remains of centuries of civilization slumbered in a macabre organization, a foundation of death supporting the life of the city above.

"My word, Holmes, have you ever seen anything like it before?"

"I can't say that I have."

We continued, the passageways twisted like the coils of a serpent, each turn revealing walls stacked high with the skeletal remains of countless souls. Bones are laid to reinforce each other in interlocking rows. Skulls interspersed neatly within the rows peered out from their resting places, seemingly grinning with wide open black eyes, their empty sockets following our every move.

The walls became closer and the tunnel narrower, the oppressive weight of the earth above pressing down on my mind. The flickering light from Holmes' lantern revealed more columns made from human femurs, pillars of the forgotten dead standing sentinel-like in the gloom.

Now the air was noticeably cooler and heavy with the scent of decay and damp limestone, an ancient staleness that clung to my throat like a vise. The faintest echo of footsteps returned to us. At first, I thought they were our own, distorted by the labyrinthine network of tunnels, but it was as though another presence walked in time with us, unseen but always near.

We continued, until the corridor of human bones opened into a chamber where the remains were arranged in spirals, twisting inward like some horrific vortex and in the center of the room stood an altar made entirely of skulls, each resting perfectly atop the other, forming a grotesque pyramid.

"An alter Holmes, like Chislehurst!"

"We are close to our answer, Watson."

Then everything was quiet. The silence was suffocating, broken only by the drip of unseen water and our hearts' slow, rhythmic beating, which seemed to grow louder in the stillness. We had come to a halt, but somewhere ahead, footsteps started again, slowly crunching upon the crumbs of limestone rock and decaying bone.

Suddenly, crackling like lightning in the air, a voice close enough to smell the corrosion of its breath boomed through the labyrinth.

"Welcome. Master expects you."

17

BONES

Holmes thrust out his left hand, complete with a lantern which swung like a hypnotist's pendulum, to halt my step. His other hand instinctively reached for the revolver in his jacket and, in one movement, pulled it clear of the pocket.

"Wait." Holmes whispered, then gestured for me to follow closely. We inched our way step by step into a chamber to emerge into an open room through what seemed previously a solid wall of bones.

Holmes raised the lantern at shoulder height to its position in front of our path. Fingers of amber light pierced the darkness, creeping slowly across the face of an unsettling design. Grotesque medallions of human skeletons adorned the walls like flags of victory. Set within large circles of long thigh bones, skulls gaped with open teeth filled mouths as if they were crying out for mercy. Crosses made entirely of femurs were arranged so that bleached skulls sat at their intersections.

It was then we caught sight, in the center of the room, a figure, a familiar shadow.

"It's him!" I cried and reached beneath my jacket for Van Helsing's charm, the protection against evil. I heard the click of the hammer of the revolver as Holmes pulled it backwards into position.

Before us stood the attendant, the same man who had greeted us at the entrance to the catacombs and guided us through his own instruction to this place. At first, I blamed the change in his appearance on the light, but it was more than that. He had changed. Two deep-set eyes were held in the center of what was, even in this poorly lit room, a ghastly pale complexion. His previously well-fitting uniform hung from his withered frame, now not much more than the skeletons that piled around us.

The man was bathed in a strange stillness and barely disturbed the air around him as he moved closer. His joints creaked and cracked as hinged, bone against bone. Holmes and I both stiffened as we felt his presence. A cold grip extended from where this thing stood like a hand tightening its fingers around our throats.

"Mr. Holmes," the attendant rasped, his voice as

brittle and dry as the bones lining the walls, "we have been expecting you."

Holmes, unflinching, stepped forward, his sharp gaze appraising the figure. I remained in place, close behind. I sensed that Holmes had placed his instincts on edge prior to the man's appearance, feeling something unnatural in the very atmosphere. The attendant's eyes, coated with a dull sheen, glowed faintly like a blind cat that lurked in the shadows. Awaiting the passing of unsuspecting rodents.

"You are the man who permitted us to enter," Holmes said, his voice cool and relaxed, though I could detect the faintest note of tension beneath his calm demeanor.

"I am but a messenger," the man replied, his lips curling into a smile that lifted his disheveled moustache but never reached his eyes. The grin widened in a strange satisfaction as he continued.

"My master, the Count, thanks you for accepting his invitation." At the mention of the name, a chill rippled through the chamber, as if the very walls had shuddered at the sound.

"There was no invitation!" I said.

"On the contrary, gentlemen, every step of your journey has been carefully measured and directed. From our departure from Chislehurst to the confrontation at Tower Bridge, you have been seen and directed. You were always going to end up in this place. It was only a question of when that would be. It seems that today is the day."

Holmes, however, remained unperturbed, his sharp intellect already piecing together the implications of this encounter.

"Of course, my good fellow, but why did he wait so long?" Holmes said, his teeth gritted together as though he tasted the words.

"He directs and is not to be directed by mere mortals."

"Then what of his direction?"

The attendant stepped closer, the shadows clinging to him and at the same time climbing the walls as he moved. His voice lowered to a whisper and what remained of his features began to bear a closer resemblance to the skulls pressed into the wall. Holmes raised the pistol. However, we both knew that bullets might prove useless against the form that stood before us.

"The Count bids you to cease your pursuit. These tunnels, these bones, they are but the representative of something far, far darker than even you can imagine, Mr. Holmes. Turn back now, return to your slumberous existence in London. If you do not, you will forever be regretful of your actions."

For a moment, the silence stretched, the weight of the threat hanging in the air. Holmes remained unreadable, his mind whirring behind those calculating eyes.

"And if we refuse?" I said.

"Then master shall be waiting for you. In the place where all routes end, where even the symbols of light or your feeble charms cannot protect you. The story presented to you is set."

With that, the attendant stepped backward into the shadows, his form dissolving into the darkness as if swallowed by the catacombs themselves. In an instant, he was gone, the bones seemingly closing around the space he had occupied, leaving only the echo of his final words and the stifling sense that something far more terrifying than immobile skeletons awaited us.

18

THE GAME

Holmes stood in the eerie calm of the catacombs, his heels tapping without rhythm on the stone floor. Alternate rows of bones turned from darkness to light and back again as the glow of the lantern flickered desperate shadows to grasp on the walls. I thought of the man's words and released my charm from the grip of my hand. The blood returned to my palm and with it the pain of feeling.

The corridors echoed the distant drip of water on decaying remains. The sound of a centuries-old torture. Holmes, his gaze fixed on the area where the attendant vanished, supped in a deep breath of cold air. His brows furrowed as his mind searched for an explanation for what they had just experienced.

"Holmes," I whispered, "Dracula is aware of our

journey. The warning, what is to do?"

"We do what we came here to do, Dr," he breathed; I could barely hear his words, which rasped against the uniform racks of femurs. "The Count has taken a direct interest in our movements over the past months. This fact is now confirmed as though we didn't realize it beforehand. Important, but not new to us or one which progresses our investigation."

"This is different, Holmes; he has been dormant for years. Why is he taking an interest now?"

"A diversion, Watson. His message reveals it was not us he was trailing," Holmes said.

"I don't understand. He had each of us followed on different occasions."

"We were but innocent bystanders to his plan, Watson."

"You mean Quincey?"

"Not at all, my dear fellow; Dracula was interested in the work of British Intelligence and the mechanisms around it. Quincey was a witness only by association. A link between Queen Victoria and Dracula's plans," said Holmes.

"The Queen is a link," I asked.

"Think, Watson, of the variety and purpose of the items taken to her grave, a protection against his darkness, Watson."

"But Dracula's man followed me as well. Explain that if you will."

"Your destination?"

"Baker Street, of course. From your telegram," I said.

"Think on. Then who and what was at Baker Street at the time of your arrival?"

"Berr..." I said, my words trailing off on the realization.

"Yes, and the book, Watson."

"The book of the great war?"

"Yes, Dracula's war. His aim is to remove any obstacle to his domination of the world."

"I'm uncertain that it is, Holmes," I said. "We are walking into a trap. Into a box already designed, with sides and a lid where logic and reason hold no sway."

"What did you expect from the Count?" Holmes chose not to address the question directly to me, but his voice, now booming through the tunnels, grumbled with irritation.

"This is precisely why we must continue. The disguised threat serves only to confirm that we are on the right path. Dracula fears discovery. He has a fear of us. Remember, we have defeated him twice."

Holmes returned the revolver slowly to its position in his jacket pocket, then placed the lantern on the floor and between his feet. A willowy shadow of the detective's silhouette positioned in thought stretched along the passageway behind him.

"But there's a difference about this time. The other cases involving Dracula were dangerous enough. This is something far darker, something beyond reason; he seeks revenge," I said.

Holmes clasped his hands behind his back, wringing them together. He remained motionless as he considered the puzzle before us. A rumbling from deep in his stomach resonated in his voice as he spoke.

"Fear, Watson. Our most formidable adversaries use it, but none as skillfully as Dracula. Revenge is the undoing of all plans. He seeks to unnerve us, to cloud our judgment.

The Count is centered on facilitating a disastrous continental war. His operation extends through many countries, and his associates are many. But suppose, Watson, we maintain our powers of deduction and logic. In that case, we have proven that Dracula is as vulnerable as any criminal we have ever encountered.

"Holmes, if Dracula wanted to use his menace to deflect us, then why lure us forward? Surely, it would serve him better to leave us lost here, bury our bones in a place where their addition would be but an acorn floating in an ocean, so to speak. Two more nicely polished skulls in the stack," I said, wrapping my knuckles on the nearest bone in the catacomb wall.

He paused, then turned to face me. Hands now shifted to be clasped together beneath his chin.

"Although the Count urges us to cease, using the catacombs as a theatrical backdrop for his warnings only encourages me to follow further. Maybe he predicts that."

"Then, if we proceed. We will be confronted by one or more members of Dracula's cult."

Holmes raised an eyebrow, his lips curling into a wry smile.

"Then we shall dispose of them and play the game at hand, Watson, as we have on previous occasions. Dracula may shroud himself in ancient myth, but beneath that veil, he is susceptible to injury. Once we have uncovered how he intends to carry out his plan, we will be better armed to sabotage his reign of fear."

Holmes turned away, twisting his whole body on his heels as though he had heard something behind him. The soft glow of the lantern illuminated his sharp features.

I furrowed my brow, unsure where Holmes was leading.

Holmes's eyes narrowed and gleamed, the pieces of Dracula's plan falling into place in his mind.

"The Count wants us to follow, but has us think we make that decision through our own deduction. He's not trying to hide from us; he's guiding us. His servant's appearance was no mere coincidence. It was a deliberate step in Dracula's game. By sending us this message, he put in place a reason to pique my curiosity and compel me to seek him out. These catacombs send a direct challenge and a backdrop for us to fight against our own fate. The Count's direction is to challenge us to overcome our own mortality. That alone tells us there is something he expects we will find elsewhere." Holmes said.

"Then there is more to this than only following his lead?" I asked, the chill of realization creeping up my spine.

Holmes shuffled, his voice calm but tinged with the weight of what he had uncovered.

"Dracula's designs are not bound to Paris. The catacombs were merely the first stage, a test of our resolve, perhaps, or mere breadcrumbs, to lure us into his clutches. His true plan lies beyond these tunnels. He wants us to pursue him into greater danger, into a trap of his own making,

"He'll make it difficult, but I suspect only in appearance, Watson. Dracula wants us, more than that desires us, to board the train for Budapest. That's where he has decided to dictate the terms of our confrontation. In his mind, this is one move of the game," said Holmes.

"The express? You believe we will be in greater danger on the train?" I said.

Holmes nodded. "Indeed. The journey will be fraught with threats, both seen and unseen. Dracula's plans are in place. His followers are waiting for us on that train. The journey to Budapest is as important as the destination itself. Dracula's strength lies not only in his power but in his ability to manipulate our path."

A silence hung between us, the realization of what awaited sinking in.

"And yet," Holmes continued, his voice steady, "you know that he underestimates us. He believes he controls the game, but that is where he errs. We shall board the train, Watson, and travel to Budapest. Dracula's arrogance will be his undoing, for he believes himself invincible."

"You have supreme confidence, Holmes," I said. "lead the way."

With a firm nod, Holmes stepped back in the direction whence we came. "Come, Watson. The game is again afoot, and Dracula, it seems, has just raised the stakes."

As we turned, the glow of the lantern reflected on an object. The sudden glint caused us both to stop in our tracks.

"My word, Holmes, a hand!" I said in amazement.

A skeleton hand of bones protruded from the face of the passage wall between a line of femurs. The shadows cast by the lantern gave the form life. Its sharp, bony fingers curled upward and grasped for release. But there, on the third finger, was a golden ring. Holmes reached out and plucked it from its position.

I was afraid that someone had rigged the jewelry as a booby trap, and I had concerns that the walls would collapse on us. It wasn't, and Holmes held the ring between his thumb and index finger towards the light. The gold glowed as the dark sockets of the skulls observed our find from their internment and smiled in approval.

"Now we have three." He said with a mischievous grin.

19

BOARDING

We emerged from the darkness of the catacombs into daylight through the same doorway we had entered. The dim light of the underground space was replaced instantly with the burning brightness of the late afternoon sky. Even though the sun was low and obscured by clouds, it felt like I was looking directly into the burning orb with wide-open eyes.

"It's still daylight," I said.

We stumbled through the doorway and were met with a look of utter surprise. Now, a different attendant stood in our way. His eyes widened in shock, and his mouth opened in an oval-shaped gape of disbelief.

Holmes immediately placed his free hand on the bulging pocket containing the revolver, ready for any unexpected turn of events.

The lantern, now useless, swung unevenly like an

unwanted appendage from his still-extended arm until it was released to clatter onto the stone path. Could this man be another of Dracula's messengers? Was he a companion to the man who had dissolved into the shadow's catacombs only moments before?

"What on Earth! How did you arrive here?" The new attendant exclaimed in high-pitched French. His face twisted with surprise and fear before he stood to one side.

"By carriage, my good man!" Holmes quipped as he and I galloped past the stunned attendant, simultaneously brushing the dust of rotten bones from our clothing. Seeing our carriage waiting as instructed was a comforting sight amid the uncertainty. It was a reassuring sign that we were still in control of our journey despite the mysterious events unfolding around us.

"3:35, Gare de l'Est, rapide." Holmes directed the driver in his best French to get to the station as fast as possible. The driver understood and clipped the horse with his stick. The horse took off at a brisk trot, and we were thrown into seats.

"We were down there much longer than it appeared, Holmes," I said as we settled into a more upright position.

"Yes, a compounding of time, somehow."

"Not too compounded to distract us from dinner," I said.

"As you say, Watson, there is time enough to refill our tanks."

"Driver, to a restaurant as close to the station as possible, if you please," Holmes said.

"The best food," the driver responded.

We arrived at the restaurant without further incident, a welcome relief after the mysterious events. We had little more than three hours to wait before we could board the train, giving us a moment of respite.

"Café Américain?" I said, with a degree of disappointment. I was further non-plussed when a table was found.

However, despite its name and my prejudice, the restaurant served many excellent-quality French dishes. As I worked my way through the main course, the aroma of my roasted leg of lamb with asparagus jolted my mind back to the harlequin vendors we had passed earlier in the day. Something struck me, something familiar. It was then that I realized.

"Holmes, I recall something."

"I hope it is more than your own name, Dr."

"Really, Holmes!"

"You are thinking of earlier in the day, outside the station, Watson, as we hurried for the carriage."

"Why yes, the porter Holmes, the porter who nearly took my foot off."

"I put it together as soon as you suffered the encounter."

"But how, Holmes?"

"The socks, Watson, the red socks."

"I did see the flash of red, but it did not register until now. He was also an associate of Dracula, wasn't he?"

"Following our steps from Charing Cross to Paris."

"My word, Holmes. They are everywhere!"

"All around us, Watson."

After enjoying our last taste of Paris, we gathered and marched towards the Gare de l'Est railway station. The building's stature reflected its importance as the entrance to the East. Its arched façade was adorned with classical architectural embellishments. Once inside, we were overwhelmed by the terminus, bustling with the footsteps and chatter of Europe's elite.

"The gateway to Eastern Europe and perhaps to Dracula's kingdom," I murmured.

"Welcome, Mr. Holmes and Dr. Watson. I recognize you from your description in the London press. We have your accommodation ready," a voice with only the faintest of accents said as he approached.

Immediately in our path, standing almost to attention, was a tall, well-groomed bearded man. His dress was impeccable: a dark blue double-breasted jacket and matching cap embroidered on its face with intricate gold piping. His tailored uniform held golden epaulets and was fastened with bright gold buttons. A small badge on his chest was marked 'Chef de Train.' This man was the ticket master.

"Yes, you have us correct," I replied.

"Gentlemen, may I introduce myself? I'm Auguste Martineau, the chef de train, and I will guide you through the boarding process. Let's get you started, shall we? First, your tickets, please."

I searched the inside pocket of my jacket, my fingers at first, finding only a pen and my passport. A quick rummage to the very bottom of the fabric eventually found the tickets. I pulled them out with a flourish that befitted a concert pianist. Holmes exchanged greetings with monsieur Martineau while casting an eyebrow-raised silent glance in my direction. The ticket master paid little notice as he stamped our boarding passes and deposited their stubs into a small brown leather satchel that hung tightly at his side,

"Platform 1, there she is, gentlemen," Said Martineau.

My eye caught the badge, an emblem, on Martineau's cap. At the heart of the symbol stood a pair of majestic lions facing each other in a regal stance. The lions held a shield between them, emblazoned with the initials "CIWL" and rendered in a sophisticated script, which shimmered in gold against a backdrop of the deep royal blue of the cap. Encircling the lion and the shield was a richly detailed garland of laurel leaves crafted in gold, a mark of prestige and excellence.

"Our luggage?" I asked.

"Already transferred and loaded into the baggage car," said Martineau.

My eyes widened as I turned towards the train and caught the elegance of the sleek black and blue carriages. The train stood there like a majestic beast. Its glossy surface reflected the station lamps in narrow white ribbons, like lightning strikes across a tempestuous sky.

Twisting together like coiling snakes, white plumes of steam and smoke rose and dissipated into the cool night air. As they boarded, the passengers' thoughts were on the adventure of the train. They had no concern and carried little other than their luggage with them. They had no idea they would not reach their destination.

The dining car exuded an air of almost royal grandeur. Stacks of cases and heavy trunks sat on carts waiting to be loaded. Their leather surfaces were embossed with various initials and crests. Some bore the marks of multiple journeys, others were new to adventure.

As we passed open carriage doors, the scent of fine leather and polished wood wafted faintly into the air, mingling with the steam and harsh odor of coal. By preliminary observation of the platform, the train had a full complement of passengers from all parts of high society.

Holmes moved forward, his eyes never ceasing their restless survey of the crowd, the carriages, and the multitude of uniformed staff. Pausing at the side of the center carriage of the Express, he gazed at the Companie Internationale des Wagons-Lits emblem.

The attendants, immaculate in their navy-blue uniforms trimmed with gold braid, stood at attention by the doorways, ready to welcome all the passengers. Unmarked, white-gloved hands held the doors open.

"A fine piece of machinery, Holmes," I remarked quietly.

"Certainly Watson. Although it is built to carry passengers, this train also carries the weight of Dracula's scheme. Mark it well; this journey is a stage upon which the drama of Europe is set to play out."

Indeed, as we stood before this magnificent train, its many mysteries seemed to hum beneath the thin veneer of luxury, waiting for the moment when this man-made serpent would begin its lurch eastward, across borders, and into the heart of Europe's intrigue. Monsieur Martineau reached into his satchel and pulled out a sealed envelope.

"I'm sorry, Mr. Holmes. I almost forgot to hand this to you."

20

TELEGRAM

Martineau placed the small envelope into Holmes' hand. We thanked the ticket master for his assistance and were directed by the sleeper car attendant to our carriage door. I followed Holmes as he boarded the train.

"A telegram, Holmes," I said.

"Watson, these deductive skills continue to astound the whole of Europe."

"Enough of this so-named wit, Holmes. Come, reveal the content."

"First to our cabins," Holmes said, emphasizing the need for privacy. "Privacy is the order of the day."

The attendant's gloved hand directed us to our respective cabins. I was in cabin number three, and Holmes was in cabin four. After a quick calculation, I found that our car had ten cabins in total.

In the center of each door, a permanent oval brass plaque with a stylish engraving displayed the compartment number; underneath, a small replaceable strip of gold-edged cream-colored card called out the occupant's name. I glanced below the marker of cabin two as I passed. The name 'Robertson' was written without any flaws in flowing handwriting. Then, I realized that the card gave no indication of the occupant's physical identity or gender.

The door of cabin three opened without a sound. It turned perfectly on its well-oiled hinges as I pushed the brass handle set into its wooden panel. Inside, I was greeted by the finest decoration. Rich mahogany panels complemented the plush velvet burgundy-colored upholstery. This cabin must have traveled thousands of miles across Europe since it first came into use. Yet, there was no indication or trace of any previous occupants. The room and its contents were unmarked.

I studied the plush interior. Polished paneled walls reflected the steady golden glow of the three brass lamps spaced about the room. One of the lamps sat on a small glass-topped table, under which sat my case, transferred as we had asked from the Boulogne to Paris train on our arrival today. The events stretched the day beyond our hours in the city.

A full-length mirror reflected the cabin's interior,

doubling the space's appearance. I moved toward the window and guided the closed heavy velvet curtains apart, creating a narrow gap and a platform view. Outside the car, a bustling mix of passengers and guards scurried about. I caught sight of the ticket master, Martineau. I remembered with a jolt the telegram and my requirement to join Holmes in its opening.

I left my cabin, secured the door, and turned towards where Holmes was housed. For a moment, the passageway along the carriage was empty save the equally spaced rows of cabin doors on either side. Then that's when I first saw it. A dark shadow swept across the far end of the car; its shape was familiar to me, but I could not place it. A cold chill placed its fingers across my face, and the lamplight flickered. Then the shape was gone, even though there was nowhere for it to go. I steadied myself and continued a few paces along the corridor, knocking on the varnished door of cabin four. My silhouette reflected before me.

"Holmes, it's me, Watson."

"Enter Dr."

Apart from Holmes reclining somewhat sanguinely on the velvet seat, the cabin in appearance was identical to my own. His legs were crossed with the upper kicking in an impatient rhythm. The unopened telegram played impatiently between the fingers of his left hand. His opened pocketknife in his right.

"Hmm, there we are, Watson." He said, giving a concentrated stare through raised eyebrows and tapping the blade against his knee.

"I was settling in."

"It's not a rest house, Watson; we have work to do."

"Of course, Holmes, I was..." I said, but he leaped upright to stand at the small table before I could finish.

Holmes continued to revolve the telegram between his fingers like the beginning of a deft origami demonstration. His eyes scrutinized the envelope before laying the item on the tabletop. The wax seal faced upwards. Holmes took the pocketknife's blade, laid it flat, and slid it expertly through the underside of the seal. The seal broke. The flap of the envelope popped open. Reaching his fingers inside, Holmes withdrew the single folded sheet of thin off-white paper and opened it to read.

"What does it relay, Holmes?"

"It's from Quincey."

"It says **LONDON NEWSPAPERS REPORT ANARCHISTS GATHERING.**"

"My word, Holmes, could this be part of the group summoned by Dracula?" The mere mention of Dracula sent a shiver down my spine. The mere thought of a connection to such a notorious figure was terrifying.

"We will discover their purpose soon enough, Watson. This is indeed an ember that is set to glow. Request the car attendant obtain a copy of the English press." Holmes' tone was urgent, his eyes focused and determined, leaving no room for delay.

"I shall do that with urgency," I said.

As Holmes nodded in approval, he returned to the velvet seat, his fingers absentmindedly tracing the intricate pattern of the upholstery. He continued to consider the entire cabin.

"This train, Watson, is a fitting environment for those who believe they have left the world of ordinary men behind; they may not be far wrong. Be quick about it. Others are already in motion."

I left in a hurry to find the sleeper attendant. I found the man in conversation with the occupant of cabin two, 'Robertson.' The attendant was standing at the cabin door, which was slightly ajar. Still, by no more than an inch, the occupant remained behind the door and hence unseen as they conversed.

"Breakfast is served from 7:00. I shall ensure that your table is secured," said the attendant before the door closed, and the young man turned to face me. He was a striking figure, with a neat, well-manicured mustache that hung below a substantial nose. His uniform was worn with a pride that suggested this was his first job, and his smile seemed to confirm my assumption.

"Can I help you, sir?" he said with only a hint of an accent. I read from the polished gold badge pinned to his chest.

"Yes, you may, monsieur Laurent. I require your assistance in obtaining a copy of the London papers of today's date." The sleeper car attendant glanced at his watch.

"The papers will have been delivered only this evening by a special courier. They will be in the lounge. Please follow me, sir."

Laurent guided me through the carriages to the lounge car, where a rack held all the London papers together with papers from all over Europe. I thanked the attendant and asked.

"Do we need to reserve tables for breakfast? I could not help but overhear your conversation with the passenger in cabin two."

"You will have a table already allocated. It is only if you have a special request to be seated in a certain location in the dining car."

"Ah, no, that won't be necessary, but thank you for your help."

I brought the stack to Holmes' cabin and, without

hesitation, spread them on the desk.

Then we found it. Buried amongst the news from Europe on an inner page, a small headline taking no more than an eighth of a column appeared the following:

ASSASSINATION PLOT

21

THE PLOT

Holmes remained bent at the desk, glancing through the article, running his index finger horizontally through the lines at speed. He straightened himself up, glanced at the ceiling, and returned to his seat. His face was a study of great concentration.

I'm sure he would have picked his violin from its worn case and plucked at its strings if he could. However, the instrument was out of reach, awaiting his return at Baker Street. Holmes said no more. I maneuvered the page in my direction and held it in front of me as I started to read aloud. I wandered about the confined space of the cabin as my own concentration gained momentum.

"*ASSASINATION PLOT: SIGHTING OF FUGITIVE ANARCHIST LUIGI BOSCHETTI*"

"*Budapest Monday: Notorious Italian anarchist Luigi Boschetti was reported to have been sighted by authorities in Budapest. Boschetti, whose name has become synonymous with the rising tide of violent revolutionary movement across Europe, has eluded capture for nearly a year and is now believed to be orchestrating anarchist activity from the heart of the Hungarian capital.*"

"*Boschetti, a prime candidate to be a part of this, don't you surmise Holmes?*" I asked.

"*Circumstantial connection is a very tricky thing,*" said Holmes, "*It may seem to adhere to the consequence which we seek, but if you reposition your own point of view a little, you may find it points to something entirely different. I must confess, however, that the connection has some merit.*"

"*I should say it has,*" I said and continued to read.

"*An informant claims to have seen the anarchist entering the Red Frog Tavern in the Castle District, a neighborhood known for keeping its secrets to itself. According to a police spokesman, the witness described Boschetti as being 'agitated and nervous.'*"

"Not the demeanor of a vital member of Dracula's cult, would you say, Watson?" Holmes said.

"He was attempting to conceal his identity though, but

listen to this, the distinctive scar on the side of his neck gave him away."

"You are thinking that the scar is the mark of Dracula?"

"An obvious link. We have seen such indentations before, Holmes."

"With our own eyes, Watson. The mark could easily be a healed cut, a blemish from birth, or a childhood accident. You are leading yourself along, perhaps down, the wrong path. We need more information on the matter. I'm interested in the man heading the investigation, Dr?"

"Yes, here. Inspector József Kovács says Boschetti is a highly dangerous individual with connections to European anarchist networks. His presence in Budapest is part of a larger plot threatening Hungary and the region's stability. You see, Holmes, the police themselves detect a larger plot."

Holmes jolted upright. Something from the depths of his memory had returned to him. He drew back the curtains and studied the platform. Most passengers had by now boarded the train. A streaming carpet of steam filled their footsteps. The express was ready to commence its journey. I could see the reflection of his face in the glass. His brow furrowed, as it did when he found some small piece of the puzzle.

"The plot in London!" Holmes exclaimed.

"What plot?"

"I recall the connection of this name to several bombings and assassination attempts that were happening all over Europe. Summer last year, there was a threat aimed at a member of the British royal family. It involved a member of the family that is not in full public view or visibility. Lestrade informed me the plot had been resolved before we were called into the investigation."

"You have me at a disadvantage, Holmes. You say that this was the same man?"

"I believe so, Watson."

Holmes drew back the curtains and returned to the chair. I returned my attention to the article.

"Boschetti's arrival in Budapest appears to coincide with the growing political unrest in the city. There are concerns that the anarchist's activities are focused on destabilizing the Austro-Hungarian monarchy. There is a suggestion that a high-profile assassination may be imminent."

"Hmm. We know there is already a much broader conspiracy involving other anarchist cells throughout Europe. This man is part of a wider group of anarchists from Italy. He has many associates, including Gaetano Bresci, the assassin who killed King Umberto during a scheduled appearance in Monza. The group has also been linked to the assassination of the Persian king Mozaffar ad-Din

Shah Qajar in Paris, the murder of Empress Elisabeth of Austria, and an attempt upon the life of the Prince of Wales at Brussels railway station."

"So, this is the alignment with the book delivered to Baker Street by Bellinger and then ultimately with Dracula?"

"Of that, I am not certain. Whether the anarchist group is already aligned, planned to be, or has no connection is the question to be answered."

"But Holmes, all of this accumulates to point towards a conspiracy already agreed and in operation."

"Again, Watson. I urge you to apply for calmer thought. There is more to find, much more."

Holmes retrieved a small pad of notepaper and a pen and scribbled two messages. He handed them to me, and in a steady voice, he said.

"We need more information, Watson. Before the train departs, send these as telegrams: one for Quincey and this one for Lestrade. We will collect the replies in Vienna."

22

THE TIDE

The concierge was a small, round man about five and a half feet tall. His uniform fit tighter than it should, and he was in the first-class lounge when I found him. This car had an air of opulence built into every fabric of its interior. The lounge was filled with light. Chandeliers hung from its ceiling, complemented by decorative brass sconces. A few passengers were already partaking in drinks and engaged in whispered conversations. I delivered the messages.

"These two telegrams need to be sent tonight. It's urgent," I stressed to the concierge, the gravity of the situation evident in my tone. The importance of the task was not lost on him, and he nodded in understanding.

The concierge, with a practiced hand, retrieved a silver

pocket watch from his waistcoat. The fabric stretched and groaned as he pulled it out, the watch popping into his hand like a cork from a champagne bottle. Flicking it open in the palm of his hand, he glanced at the instrument, closed it, shifted his cap to one side, and then wriggled the watch back into its home.

"Certainly, sir. I can have them go before we leave the station," the concierge assured me in an excellent version of English, his tone reflecting the urgency of the task, before hurrying out of the lounge door and down its steps onto the platform.

It was then that my attention was caught by a man sitting at the far end of the lounge. It was the wine buyer who I had met on the crossing, Guinness. He waved his hand in a gesture to join him. Green sat beside him, his face the same pallor he wore on the ship, a damp, whitewashed, waxy grey. They both had drinks in hand. Guinness sipped his whiskey on ice, and Green stared into a glass of red wine, which was hardly touched.

"I shouldn't have had those oysters," Green murmured as a burbling sound erupted from his belly. He rubbed at his stomach with a vigorous circular motion of his hand, his discomfort palpable. "I think I had better make my excuses. Leave you gentlemen to it, and return to my cabin before we get underway." He gathered himself, shook my hand, and wobbled towards, then stumbled through the exit.

"He certainly won't enjoy the rocking of the carriage in the state he's in," I said.

"Made the mistake of taking some food from the vendors at the station," Green informed. "Dr. Watson, you have an urgent business, I see?" He pointed towards the concierge as he made his way through the remaining passengers waiting to board.

"Well, just a couple of messages back to London, nothing of great importance," I replied, attempting to disengage from the matter.

"Maybe you should have told him that," he nodded towards the concierge, who was now running along the platform with my messages in hand.

"We should be underway in a moment; I think that's his hurry," I said; Guinness smirked.

"You called me Dr. I don't recall that I had introduced myself so?"

"I'm sure you did. How on earth would I know such a thing?"

"Hmm, quite so."

"Join me for a drink; I hear they do a spiffing sherry."

"Maybe later or tomorrow, I must meet with my companion."

"That's unfortunate. Well, we should try that. In any case, you are on your way to Budapest, and I was hoping that we could meet there after I have finished my business with the wine merchant. Where will you be staying?"

"We have not decided as yet."

"I'm staying at the hotel ... I'm sure they will have rooms if you require. I can telegram ahead if needed."

"That's awfully kind of you, but we will make our own arrangements. It was good to see you. Hopefully, we will align our timetables tomorrow."

"It's very likely. After all, there's no other place we can go, right?"

"Quite," I said and made my leave.

I returned to cabin four of the sleeper car one. He was not relaxing as anticipated, but bending across the desk with his palms flat. The newspaper was open, but I noticed it was now folded in a different article. He was reading the text with the concentration of a snake charmer.

"They are transmitted, Holmes; I suspect we shall have a reply waiting for us at Vienna."

Holmes did not respond. Instead, his demeanor became rigid, his whole being fixed on the newspaper. Then, I read the title of the article.

"A STRANGE TIDE SPREADS ACROSS EUROPE. What is it Holmes?"

Holmes withdrew to his chair and took a position that was too familiar. He sat forward with his chin cupped with both hands. A position that I knew meant there was a complication or fact that would need to be resolved before we could complete the analysis. I returned my attention to the newspaper and read it aloud.

"*Reports of a wave of grave robberies sweeping from Paris to Budapest are both mystifying and terrifying local people. The populations of several major cities have been left in a state of total alarm. What began as a series of seemingly unconnected incidents in Paris has now spread eastward to most major cities. With disturbing evidence of desecrated graves emerging from Berlin, Brussels, Vienna, Prague, and most recently, Budapest.*" *I paused, glanced at Holmes, then continued.*

"*Detective Herbert Kessler of the Berlin Kriminalpolizei said, 'These disturbances do not seem motivated by greed. As far as we are aware, nothing of value has been taken. When we are able, we interview relatives of the deceased. All reports show that there were no missing items from what was recovered at the site of the grave. Except for the body itself, that is. The families took small comfort from being reconnected with personal mementos, such as engravings and medals given in battle. They are very distressed by the whole thing.'*

'*The violations are targeted, with specific individuals seemingly singled out for unknown reasons. The lack of a clear motive only added to the situation's perplexity, making the reason even deeper to fathom.'*

"Kessler denied reports of strange symbols being found near the graves.

"In Budapest, inspector József Kovács also commented on the nature of the crimes: 'We are dealing with a calculated and well-organized operation.'

"Some darker whispers suggest that the grave robbers could be involved in the recent resurgence of anarchist activity across Europe. However, no anarchist groups have claimed responsibility, and the political motivations behind such actions remain speculative.

"Until the culprits are apprehended, the answer as to the reason for the widespread desecration will remain buried, unlike the stolen dead they remove."

"My word, Holmes, do you think these events are connected with the movement of anarchists?"

"Certainly, we know very well the subtle methods by which Dracula employs his influence. His way of using carefully directed whispers to reach into the minds of those most easily manipulated. He may have begun his plot by targeting the leaders of the anarchist cells. Those having the ability to mobilize others are already consumed by rage against the ruling classes.

"You mean Boschetti?"

"Yes, but more importantly, the followers of Boschetti. Visiting the rogues in their dreams. The Count will already be meeting them, charming them. He will present himself as an ally of their cause, a wealthy benefactor with deep-rooted ties to the underworld. A man with resources ready and able to assist in their revolutionary dogma.

"The reports of meetings in Budapest!"

"Yes, Watson, the wheels are in motion. We are unlikely to be able to stop the anarchists. But, most importantly, I think that Dracula will not take ownership of the plot until it is close to finality."

"How do we stop this, Holmes?"

"The only way to stand a chance is to keep moving. We all journey eastward, Watson. The issue is that we tread in the footsteps of others and are not yet ahead of the scheme."

23

ENCOUNTER

I returned to my cabin, my mind disturbed by thoughts of anarchists dabbling in the dark arts. The thought of these sinister forces working together sent shivers down my spine. I only relaxed somewhat after securing the door behind me as soon as possible, the oiled brass latch issuing a satisfying click. The cabin's polished finishes and velvet materials gave the space a homely, warming glow. Now more relaxed, my mind began to clear as I moved to the small table in the corner, which, for this journey, would act as my writing desk.

No sooner had I set out my luggage and retrieved my journal than I heard the shrill departure whistles and cries of "Tous à bord, all aboard!"

The carriages jerked and strained at their couplings.

The train pulled away from the station, leaving a cloud of steam in its place. The carriage rocked back and forth, reverberating with comforting and hypnotic chatter. As I smoothed the pages open with the back of my hand, I noticed my palms were sweaty. After wiping them dry with my handkerchief, I began to write.

My pen glided across the paper, a dreamlike summary of the day's events. But it had not been a dream; our interactions had the appearance of a nightmare. The more I thought about our experience, the greater the night and tiredness pulled at my eyelids. I slid my notebook back into its place in my briefcase.

A sense of unease crept over me like a shadow in the night, and I felt the advance of impending danger. The luxurious interior of the carriage, with its plush seats and golden brass fittings, was a stark contrast to the dark thoughts swirling in my mind. But I felt sleepy. I inched my way towards the carriage window in slow motion. I drew back the curtains to reveal the full extent of the window, almost as though opening a door. The dark of the night was interrupted by the waning lights of the outskirts of Paris as they flashed by.

I caught sight of my reflection. A tired and unshaven face stared back with blank eyes. The rhythm of the carriage wheels on the rails and the flickering lights of distant farmhouses washed against my tiredness. It was like I was being hypnotized towards the warmth of a velvet cocoon.

During my absence from the cabin, the sleeper car attendant had converted the seat into a bed. I lay on it without undressing, curled up, and drifted towards the edge of sleep. The cabin became quiet, a disturbing stillness of air and sound. It felt like someone had placed a hand in the center of my chest, taking my breath and pressing me down into the mattress. I was alone, isolated in this eerie silence, with only the sound of the train as my company.

The golden radiance of the brass lamps diminished to a faint ember, their light dancing as if manipulated by an unseen presence. Outside, the night pressed against the glass, a dense blackness unbroken by the passing countryside. Then, with my eyes closed, I heard the faintest of whispers, only a breath, yet there was no mistake. It was there, a sound that curled like smoke through the narrow space of the cabin.

Then I opened my eyes, and from the ether, they began to coalesce into view.

Initially, it was nothing, just a flicker in the shadows, something unnatural. I felt the hairs on my arms and back of my neck bristle with unease. Then, the swirling mass began to emerge against the mirror, the glass opening as a door. I couldn't move. Blurred by tiredness, my eyes struggled to focus on the apparitions that formed. Then, from the shadows, they appeared, one by one, transparent but undeniably there.

Three women, each as pale as moonlight, their forms shifting and manipulating the air about them. Delicate and translucent silk robes clung to their figures like a second skin, whispering in the air as they moved. Their eyes, glowing with a predatory hunger, pulsating red like embers of a dying fire. Their beauty was otherworldly, a sight that both mesmerized and terrified me.

"Who are you?" I said, my voice no louder than a sigh and my breath weak.

The pressure on my chest increased, a weight that further stilled my breath. My limbs were frozen where they lay. I was both terror-stricken and paralyzed, as if someone had drugged me. My heart pumped with a heavy, slow thump. I attempted to avert my eyes from the apparitions with all my will, but my strength betrayed me. Their unearthly beauty pulled my spirit towards their control. I screamed for help, but my voice was no louder than a whisper, lost in the haunting melody that filled the cabin.

The woman at the forefront stepped closer. Her face was an exquisite mask of ghostly perfection, the flesh as pale as porcelain. There was a familiarity about her features that I could not place. Her lips, crimson and full, curved into a smile that sent a subterranean quake of fear through my very soul. She leaned closer, her breath like ice, and whispered in a soft and soulless voice.

"Poor, weary adventurer, you know who we are. Your desire is to be with us."

"No..." I tried to say, but no sound emerged from my mouth, only a weak breath. I fought against the seductive pull of their words, my willpower, the only defense I had left.

"You want us, don't you?" the woman said.

She extended her long, thin fingers and then scratched along my forearm, leaving a line of indentations on my flesh. It was like a raking comb of icicles. Although my mind urged me to break free and move my arm, I could not.

The two other women moved behind her, a sound not of footsteps but of rushing air, like the hollow echo of a seashell held against a willing ear. The train rocked, and so did I. My head moved from side to side, but my eyes remained fixed on the first woman. The others laughed in synchronicity. Then they started to sing. A low and melodic melody of temptation and death resounded within the cabin. Could no one other than me hear?

"Rest," the second woman whispered, her voice softer than the first, yet laced with a hypnotic sweetness.

She approached to be beside me, her long black hair flowing like a river of ink down her back. Her lips hovered, and I could feel the cold desire of her breath on my skin, stirring the hair on the nape of my neck.

"You have traveled far. Come, let us take you to your destination."

"Holmes…" I tried to shout.

Then the third woman, perhaps the most beautiful and terrifying of them all, stood at the foot of my bed, her eyes locked upon mine. She did not speak, but her gaze held me fast, trapping me in a web of craving and dread. The dim light flickered, casting shadows across her face, but there was no mistaking the hunger behind her smile, the hunger for life, my life.

I was overcome by a drowsiness that seemed to be summoned by their presence. I felt myself sinking into an inescapable darkness as my eyelids weighed me down like lead. The night closed in around me, and their voices became a lullaby of temptation. This melody swirled and danced in my mind, beckoning me toward the edge of oblivion.

Yet, even as my strength faded, some deeper instinct, some primal fear, surged within me. I thought of Holmes, and his words rang in my mind: 'Beware what lurks in the shadows, Watson, for there are many in this world that prey upon the unwary.'

I fought with all my strength to resist their seductive voices and the temptation to submit. With a final effort, I forced my hand to move, my fingers brushing against the cross that hung around my neck. As if stung, the women recoiled, their eyes widening in sudden fury. The air crackled with static electricity.

Their faces twisted into masks of rage, their smiles vanishing as their voices turned venomous. They hissed like serpents deprived of their prey. But I stood my ground, Van Helsing's token of protection giving me strength.

"You cannot evade us," growled the first one, her eyes burning with a crimson fire. "We will find you and take you to our master. When he is over you, you will beg for the release of death."

And then, just as quickly as they had come, they were gone. The cabin was empty. The clatter of the car on its rails and the steady rhythm of motion continued as if nothing had occurred. A stillness returned to the air. I felt my heart pounding and wiped away the cold sweat on my brow. Their sudden departure left me with a sense of relief but also a lingering unease.

I lay there, staring at the ceiling, my mind racing with what had just transpired. Were my visitors real or merely the phantoms of a troubled dream? I did not know, but one thing was sure: we were speeding eastward toward Dracula and the darkness from which those creatures had come. I grasped the token in my hand and slept.

24

INFORMERS

My eyes snapped open. Was that a knock at my door? The curtains were drawn open, and I looked up from the bed to the space between them. The dark now replaced with a cloudless morning sky. I turned my gaze to the ceiling and listened to the clock as it seemed to tick in time with the carriage, as it rocked back and forth with a reassuring permanence.

I sat up and glanced at the time, the hands showed 6:35. Outside, the flat countryside of the evening was now full of valleys. Tree covered slopes, buildings and the outskirts of a town, blurred by speed, flashed by. The darkness of the night's events, a series of unsettling encounters and unexplained phenomena, was replaced by a profound sense of relief, a soothing balm washing over me like a gentle tide.

My visitors were no more, the mirror just as it should

be, now filled only with the reflection of the cabin. I reminded myself sternly to regain my sensibility and set about erasing any thought that the visit could have been anything but a dream. A dream brought on by the previous day's encounters and old memories of Jonathan Harker's journal. A document which described in chilling detail a terrifying encounter between Harker and similar mysterious figures. A double knock rapped on the door.

"Watson," Holmes said, "It's breakfast. Join me in the dining car. We have business to attend."

"Yes, dressing now. I'll be there in a moment," I replied, shocked that Sherlock was awake at such an early hour. He was, as a rule a late riser, but more stunned by the fact that I had awoken later than I had planned.

It was breakfast and I had slept through the 2 a.m. stop at Strasbourg, we had left France and entered Germany, I inspected my pocket watch. It confirmed the time, which meant that we would be entering and stopping at Munich very soon. I had missed the stop and therefore, the opportunity to observe any new passengers boarding the train.

After dressing, I checked myself in the mirror which only hours ago seemed to be a doorway to the Count himself. My reflection showed a tired and pale man. My thought jumped back to the encounter. I pulled quickly at my door to open it. The latch was engaged, and I panicked as the door refused to open, rattling against its frame. Then I realized with relief that the door was locked, which soon caused the hair on the back of my neck to raise. No one could have entered or left without my knowledge, but evidently someone had.

The corridor was empty, and I made my way to the dining car. Once there I was directed by the server to the table where Holmes was already seated with head lowered as he perused the menu. I took a look at the carriage as I made my way towards Holmes. The dining car was a long, narrow carriage lined with mahogany panels, the same rich color as the cabins. From the underside of regularly spaced wall lamps, tassels flung themselves from side to side in time with the train's clickety-click rhythm.

The breakfast tables, ordered meticulously with crystal glasses and porcelain plates, were sporadically occupied. I suspected that additional passengers would attend at a more palatable time. The smell of freshly brewed coffee and buttered croissants mingled with the faint scent of smoke finding its way from the engine, creating a thrilling feeling of lavish but industrial refinement.

The shrill clink of silver against breakfast dishes punctuated hushed conversations. A palpable sense of intrigue hung about the car as though behind each conversation lay whispered plots, secrets, and schemes that could change the course of history. It was the perfect setting for the master of deduction to observe the subtleties of human behavior, where the flick of an eye or the twitch of a hand might betray more than most would see.

"Good Afternoon, Dr," said Holmes without diverting his attention from the menu.

"It's only 6:50," I replied. "Quite a respectable time if you ask me."

"A loss of opportunity, which will not be recovered in my time."

"We have, perhaps, ten hours before Budapest, Holmes, more than enough," I said as we perused the menus.

"We shall require all available time to plan our strategy, Watson. Undoubtedly, the mastermind behind this plot will be well aware of the hour of our arrival."

"Through his informers?"

"Enough eyes to mark our every move, yet we are marooned on this train until Budapest."

"We could throw them off if we decide to alternate our route from one of the stops, say Vienna?"

"There are reasons that would be a lost cause. This is the most direct route. Any other would result in a vital delay. Our ability to intervene is delayed by at least a day, providing the Count with precious additional time to prepare. Not to mention the many spies who are at this very moment reporting our every move. A variance in our steps would not be hidden from their master for long."

"You think they are in this car right now?" I said.

"The Count's informers, Watson, are all around, either as passengers or as service."

I glanced around at the occupiers of adjacent tables. A man who was familiar to me sat by himself at a table on the left. A husband and wife, two businessmen, a somewhat scruffy man, one professional man, and two ladies, were also seated at other tables within hearing range.

At that moment, the dining car attendant arrived to take our orders. I took a cup of tea, sausages, and an omelet, and Holmes ordered two soft-boiled eggs and a coffee.

"Hmm, we'll need to keep our wits about us, Holmes."

"I have mine; I continue to hope you have packed yours!"

"I say, Holmes, your depreciation of my observational skill is becoming somewhat tiresome, old chap."

"Well, let's test it, shall we?"

"Very well, test away." I sat backward into my chair, my mind ready for the challenge. I felt the anticipation, like a hunter waiting for his prey, the thrill of the chase electrifying my senses.

"Think of the harlequin vendors lined outside the station as we left for Montparnasse and the catacombs. Describe them to me, Watson."

"The vendors, Holmes? Yes, there were four or five, as I recall."

"Be exact. That is the challenge. Were there five or four?"

I closed my eyes and let my mind's eye return to the scene.

"Five, Holmes!"

"Excellent Watson. Now, to draw out one discernable feature from each."

"As you say. The first was a round-faced, black-haired man sporting a full beard and serving a beef stew. The woman selling hot cocoa from her cart is taller than the man. She was wearing a white blouse, with her brown hair tied up in a round. The oyster seller, a young woman, seated against the wall." I paused. "Then there was the young boy, wearing a flat cap. He was selling goat cheese. And finally, the older woman standing beside a wagon of roasted chicken and soup."

"Very good, Watson. Tell me more about the oyster seller."

"What about her? She was about her normal activity,

like the others lined against her."

"Oysters, Watson?"

"I believe so."

"The woman was sniffling, her eyes outlined red, swollen, and bloodshot?"

"Possibly, now you mention it."

"What do you think would be the cause, Dr?"

"Well, the symptoms affecting her eyes could be the result of an allergic reaction, in my estimation. Why yes, like an aversion to shellfish, Holmes," I said with a start of revelation.

"Excellent diagnosis, Dr. Do you reckon that any sane person with such an affliction would be putting themselves in proximity to one of their most irritating substances without an external reason for doing so?"

"If you put it such, then there may be persuasion, Holmes."

"Or partnership. What of the other peculiarities?"

"I do not recall, minds a bit fuzzy, old man."

"Then let me provide a nudge. The knife?"

"A bladed knife for opening oysters, of course! Any person engaged in the sale of oysters would have the same."

"Markings upon the blade, then?"

I paused momentarily until the vendor's vision solidified in my mind. Then something came to me.

"Ahh, no, I can't recall any markings on the steel, Holmes. But I can recall that the long blade was attached to a carved bone grip."

"A Bowie knife, then?"

"As you say, Holmes."

"Not a locally sourced tool. An oyster vendor in Paris would use a locally refined tool. One that bears the emblem of the elephant of Thiers, the steel maker. The knife being used by the merchant was of American origin."

"American?"

"Yes, and what of the ring?"

"Well, I do recall a ring, but only that it was a heavy gold affair."

"Carrying the emblem of a double-headed eagle no less. The symbol which we are seeing as a link between members of the sect."

"My word, the same as we came across in the Catacombes today and at Chislehurst and Tower Bridge?"

Holmes sunk into his seat in satisfaction. His lips curved with the mark of a smile at their ends.

"Well, Holmes, let me tell you two observations I have made within the last day."

"You have my full attention, Watson."

"There, the man at the table immediately behind Green."

"Yes."

"He's the chap I observed disembarking from the train at Folkestone, the man with the wooden box and the unusually shaped case."

"The case and the box, Watson? Is that all you know of him?"

"Why yes, I have not yet had the opportunity to converse with the man."

"Neither have I, Watson, but I can tell you that the man is a journalist. His name is Frederic Villiers, a celebrated war artist and correspondent, and he travels to the region, maybe on information supplied to him by agencies who know more than we do."

"How on Earth, Holmes?"

"His luggage, Watson, a case-shaped to hold a typewriter, the initials upon it, F.V., the leather pads on the elbows of his jacket, the artist's box full of paints, brushes, and paper, and the variety of newspapers all folded on his table at the page of the same illustration, ready to be presented as a conversation aid at the first opportunity. Your other observation, Watson?"

Before I could answer, a young woman, whom I

estimated to be in her twenties, entered the dining car and carried herself toward the empty table immediately to our left.

"Holmes, the approaching woman, she is the one I saw on Folkestone docks."

25

PRINCESS

The woman was a vision of elegance in her tailored silk white dress. A high, lace-trimmed neckline accentuated her jawline. Her head was crowned with a white wide-brimmed hat. Her hands were encased in soft white leather gloves that extended above each elbow and remained poised at her side. A long strand of pearls draped around her neck rocked back and forth in rhythm to the carriage. She carried a small parasol, holding it by its golden handle.

Her complexion was fresh and bright. A glint of golden sunlight caught her well-defined features and reflected in her green eyes. Even though the light was piercing, she refused to squint. Caught within the light, tiny pearl earrings glistened beneath her ears. The woman stopped beside our table. Her head bowed towards Holmes with an engaging smile.

"Mr. Holmes, it is you."

Sherlock stood in an instant and bowed towards the woman.

"Princess!" He said.

I leaped in surprise as the word 'Princess' escaped into the air, the action almost tipping my chair over. I had no clue who this lady could be, but it was clear that Holmes did.

"Dr. Watson, I presume?" She said.

"I do apologize, your highness. I'm caught without knowledge, your lady."

"Allow me to introduce Princess Daisy of Pless," Holmes interjected formally, breaking the silence.

"An honor, Princess," I said.

"Thank you. Please be seated, Mr. Holmes, and you also, Dr. This is a great coincidence as I have a favor I must ask of you both."

"May I be so bold as to ask to join you? I travel with my maid and newborn Henry. As you may imagine, the conversation is not of the highest content or reference to current world issues, other than the list of latest debutantes presenting themselves at court."

"Of course, Princess. Please be seated," Holmes said, opening his palm towards the chair beside me. Princess Daisy wafted her way to stand behind the empty chair beside me. I stood and offered the seat to the Princess, who sat with the grace of a butterfly landing on a petal.

"Now, let's dispense with the 'Princess,' shall we. Daisy will be quite suitable," she said.

"As you wish then, Daisy," Holmes said. "And then, for my part, Sherlock will suffice."

"How do you two know each other?" I asked.

"If I recall correctly, I met Daisy in the summer of '87. I was visiting Devonshire House on another complicated matter," Holmes said.

"Yes, I was there for a fancy-dress ball that evening."

"And I wasn't. I gladly avoided the event through the appropriate disguise."

"I don't recall that you attended in costume, Sherlock."

"Precisely, I did not."

"How is your hand, my Lady?"

Daisy removed her left glove, pulling gently until the material revealed her delicate, thin fingers one by one. Her hand rotated so the palm faced downwards, showing several scars. Yet, her demeanor remained unwavering, a testament to her resilience.

"All healed, Mr. Holmes," Daisy said.

"Holmes, you know more than I," I said.

"As you know, Watson, I keep abreast of the newspapers. Last October, there was a report that the

Princess and her husband were injured in an accident in France as their car collided with an errant horse."

"We were traveling at night on a poorly lit road. In front of us, without warning, the horse reared out of nowhere. There was nothing we could do to avoid it," Daisy said, her voice trembling slightly as she recounted the harrowing experience. "The car careered off the road, missing the trees, thank goodness, and overturned. It was dreadful. I must have fallen unconscious when I awoke. I was laid at the side of the road. My hands must have broken the widow as they were both bandaged and soaked in blood."

"Someone rescued you?"

"Yes, there was a man. He had pulled me free and then used the sleeves of my blouse to wrap my palms and wrist. Ruined the whole thing, such a shame, a gift from President Loubet. He gave it to me at the opening of the Exposition Universelle, such a great event. Did you attend, Sherlock?"

"No, we were otherwise engaged, unfortunately."

"The driver told me later that the man appeared at the scene almost simultaneously as the accident happened. He disappeared as soon as transport arrived to take us to the hospital. I was disappointed that he wasn't identified, as I would have liked very much to show my gratitude to him," Daisy said, her voice tinged with a hint of mystery.

"It is a relief to see that you are fully recovered, Princess. You are traveling to Constantinople?"

"Why yes, the Anthony Drexel's invited us to meet there and board their magnificent steam yacht and cruise in the Black Sea."

"I'm unfamiliar with the Drexel's, but it sounds like an adventure."

"I hope so, I'm looking forward to traveling to Russia afterward. The Tzar always provides the warmest of receptions."

"How may we be of assistance in the meantime?" Homes said.

"I am deeply concerned, Sherlock, regarding the future of Europe," she confessed, her voice carrying the weight of most of the population of Europe. It was such an abrupt change of subject from her summer plans. Holmes placed both forearms on the table and leaned closer to Daisy. He looked directly into her eyes.

"You must not fear," said Sherlock, bending forward and patting the back of her hand. From where does this concern grow?"

"I travel all over the great nations and spend my time in the great courts of power. The talk I hear is quite unredacted, you know."

"I can imagine," said he, smiling.

"The more I hear, the greater that I am convinced that the leaders of the European nations need to meet each other on a regular schedule. If only they could be open with their thoughts and suspicions, they may be put at ease. In my own way, I have done all I can to make such meetings possible. My status has allowed me to visit English, French, and German politicians in their own habitat, free of political interference and ambition. But they have always sat, withdrawn into their power, waiting for the other to come to them."

"That may be the case, but what exactly have you found from your presence during such conversations?"

"The Kaiser had said the best thing would be for a treaty between England and Germany; his one desire was peace and prosperity. But to make war, and shed blood, and make orphans and widows, for the sake of his own aggrandizement would, in my eyes, make the Emperor the greatest sinner of this generation, and I told him so."

"The two most ambitious nations in partnership, how couldn't that be positive for European stability?" I said.

"But then I think, what would France and Russia say?" Daisy said.

"I imagine, Princess, they would only be delighted and feel at rest, seeing that the two had yielded to the other and had tempered German ambition. France should be relieved by such a treaty. If there was a war between Germany and England, it would be France who would be the greatest sufferer, as the war would take place in French fields and towns. Germany is not going to risk losing any ships by coming to invade the English coast; she will march to England via France." I said.

The Princess stared out of the window, and I followed her gaze. Outside, the dawn sun lit the landscape, the speed of the train smearing the green and yellow carpet like a palette knife over an oil painting. She sighed and turned to face Holmes with a resigned look.

"I know you feel it, gentlemen. I know it. The world is holding its breath. Europe is a tinderbox; one spark will ignite all the repressed ambitions and passions. War is inevitable, I fear. The leaders don't trust each other. They all seem so reckless now."

"What of your wider connections, outside of the Kaiser? Do they sense the same unrest?"

"In London, the whispers of war are stifled by diplomacy, but there is fear in their eyes. Paris is nervous. Berlin, my dear Germany, brimming with ambition, is restless. In Vienna, they speak of threats from the East, while Moscow, well, you know as well as I, gentlemen, that the Tsar is under siege by his own people. And there's Budapest..."

Daisy paused, her face becoming unsettled, and she again gazed out of the window. The speeding scenery seemed to calm her thoughts. Holmes leaned forward, his brow furrowed in an inquisitive question mark. He placed a palm on top of the Princess's gloved hand. His eyes narrowed with concern as he spoke.

"Budapest, what of Budapest?"

"Budapest, yes. I was informed by an unnamed agency that something insidious lies within the city's walls. Something which aims to corrode society."

26

ANARCHY

The brakes of the engine issued a metallic shriek as the wheels caught metal on metal. In the background, sporadic buildings of small villages which had been blurred against the backdrop of rolling pastures came into focus. We were in a more urban area, we were entering Munich. As the Express slowed further, I observed the railway station had no distinctive features to speak of, and, in fact, resembled most other rail terminals.

The platforms were protected by a vaulted roof of iron beams which supported glazed panels. The daylight filtered through, casting dappled light onto the platforms below, catching and highlighting the attendants' uniforms against dignitaries dressed in the day's fashions. Men and women milled about the station. The men dressed in long coats, the women topped with feather adorned hats over skirts of a rather voluminous outline.

As the train came to a halt at its platform, there was a hurried thrust of new passengers and porters, who headed towards the opening doors of the carriages like lemmings urged towards a cliff edge. Holmes gave a nod in my direction, which I took as an instruction to study the demarcation and boarding of passengers and, more importantly, to note their descriptions. I saw the few passengers who had left the train swallowed by the crowd as they jostled to be reunited with their luggage. Quite a melee.

With a gentle pat, Holmes released his hand from where it rested atop Daisy's, leaned backward, and closed his eyes. He had listened with the greatest concentration of his attention and was now considering the puzzle, which had added its own piece.

Daisy lowered her head and played with her pearls like a rosary. The lounge rattled, and the lamps in the carriage flickered as the train pulled away with a jerk. The breakfast plates rattled, and our drinks lapped at the edges of their cups, but not a drop was spilled.

"What more did this other agency tell?" Holmes said, half opening his eyelids and gazing at the Princess.

"They know of the assembly in Budapest. More than two dozen anarchists have been working and gathering support for months. Integrating into society, they cloak themselves in the guise of revolutionaries but are pawns in a greater game."

"We've uncovered something far more troubling and deliberate," I said, urgency lacing my voice.

"Deliberate? You suspect a greater power behind these movements?" Daisy said.

"We believe that the anarchists are manipulated by a singular, shadowy figure. One with designs far beyond political upheaval."

"You mean this midnight legend Dracula, don't you?" Daisy said and smiled, her countenance exhibiting a dismissal of the prospect.

"We've encountered him before. He's not merely folklore. Dracula is real, and his influence reaches far," Holmes said with an underlying scowl, "what better time to strike than when the world is on the brink of chaos? Budapest has become his nest, a city unaware that it rests on the edge of madness. I'm convinced the anarchists are merely distractions but they themselves suspect they are the lead of the act. We've yet to uncover fully the Count's true designs. Still, I fear they involve more than destabilizing the status quo, which everyone suspects is his aim."

"What could be greater than that?" Daisy responded.

"Princess, you said it yourself: Europe is holding its breath. And if Dracula has his way, it will be more than the war we face. It will be destruction from within, something more insidious than bullets and treaties. I fear that there is an army of untold horror whose ranks are swelling as we speak."

Daisy closed her eyes for a brief moment, gathering her thoughts. She tapped a teaspoon against the edge of her teacup. Then, she drew a deep breath before letting it go through pursed lips.

"Worse than war you say. I cannot fathom what that would entail. But I trust your deductions, Sherlock, and will do everything to assist you in your effort stop him. I can use my influence, but it will take more than whispers in high places. What is your plan, Mr. Holmes, what can I relay to help push others towards a similar conclusion?"

"There is more data to find, and without sufficient data, I cannot derive and predict the Count's or his followers' actions. When I arrive in Budapest, I intend not to engage directly, at least not at first. My goal is to ascertain the Count's true purpose. Such individuals, drawn to chaos, often reveal more in the shadows than under direct scrutiny. He knows we come, and he will set out breadcrumbs of truths and false paths in equal measure to divert us from his aim."

"You will be on a fishing expedition, Sherlock, using yourself as bait?"

"Quite so, Princess."

"I'm considering where we will be based. Perhaps a hotel where our arrival and movements can be easily observed. I believe you may have visited Budapest before, Princess, and may be of assistance having a good feel of the layout and interests of the local population."

"I have visited Budapest several times, Sherlock. I have been welcomed by the Crown Prince on many occasions. But I can't say I'm familiar with the citizens' customs or the town's heartbeat. I have stayed principally only at the royal residence."

"You arrived more than once by train, I suppose?"

"Mostly, we did, yes."

"Do you recall from your visits a hotel that would provide a central base for our activities? As I say, I need it to be known that we are in town."

"There was once a time that we met for dinner with the Frobisher's. They were on business and were staying at the Hotel Hungaria. It is a popular destination used by important foreign visitors and businesspeople. Anyone staying there would not be able to hide the fact. Indeed, the newspapers reported the Frobisher's presence and stay at the hotel in hours because they were visiting to complete a deal for the export of wool to England."

"I thought we would be taking a lower profile, Holmes," I said, somewhat confused that we would be exposing ourselves, just as Dracula wants.

"In this case, Watson, the disguise is in how our

presence is reported. We need to be fully accessible without advertising the fact ourselves. The organization that we are dealing with always hides fractures within. I'm speaking of dissenters, individuals who find it difficult to follow ideals that have come from another's mouth. They are precisely the loose ends who could be persuaded to share information and unravel this rope."

"Even so, we can't just expect them to walk into the hotel and deliver a message to our room, so how would we initiate the exchange, Holmes?"

"They would likely come to us through a third party who is known."

"Then you have someone in mind?"

"My contact in the city. An associate versed with personal experience of the dark inners of the place and the workings of the authorities. They will help us to navigate the city's underbelly and in doing so, provide a direct route to our door."

"Hmm, you have not mentioned this contact before, Holmes."

"There is time yet. You will soon be introduced. I should say though, that you do know of her through a previous case."

"Her?"

"Do you recall the Greek interpreter and the news we received from Budapest?"

"Yes…I recall the girl, the murdered couple, Holmes?

"It is good to hear that you have laid a great deal of lumber away within your brain attic, Watson."

"Yes, but I am confused. We had no communication after the poor girl had escaped following the death of her brother. Although, as I noted at the time, you did suspect there was more to the vengeful events in Budapest."

"Again, your memory does you well, Dr. The young woman telegraphed some years since. She explained how she had taken revenge against the wrongs done to herself and her brother. Yes, I did forecast the event would be a story to be told. Nonetheless, we communicated on occasion. The last time was the day of our departure."

"Ah, the telegram, but what…" I stuttered to a halt as Holmes raised his hand to stop my words. I was about to ask for the name of the young contact. I suspected he did not want that information revealed to a wider audience. He was to be right as he usually was. Having thought for a while as Holmes and I bantered back and forth, Daisy raised herself straight in her chair, cleared her throat with the tiniest cough, and said.

"This hotel is close to the center of the city."

"The Pest side of the Danube."

"Yes."

"The labyrinths?"

"In walking distance, across the chain bridge."

"Perfect, thank you for your direction, Princess."

"Labyrinths, Holmes?" I asked.

"Yes, Watson, a great network of passages lay under the castle. Large parts are unexplored, a perfect underground base for our advisory, wouldn't you say?"

"I expect so."

"You sound hesitant, Dr."

"So long as the caves are not filled with bones?" I shuddered.

"May I ask what will your indent be, after making contact with the group, that is?"

"Certainly, Princess. Once I have gathered sufficient intelligence, we will determine whether the threat can be diffused through subtle means, perhaps undermining the trust held between the anarchists, or exposing their plot to local authorities in a manner that leaves us anonymous."

"Why anonymous?"

"I would rather the Hungarian authorities take the reward, as it will help reaffirm their ability to protect their citizens and diffuse likely protests from those seeking to overturn the government."

"What if we are unable to infiltrate this group? The authorities don't seem to have much more information than we do?" said Daisy.

"Then we must confront the Count directly and expose his plan before it's too late. I've reason to believe he will not wait long to make his move in Budapest, manipulating the chaos there to sow discord across Europe. But we must tread carefully. Dracula is no ordinary foe. Watson and I know the dangers all too well."

"He is far more dangerous than any criminal or anarchist we've encountered, Princess. And if he's aligned himself with these revolutionary movements, it could mean disaster for all of Europe," I said.

"Then we will stop him. We must act before Budapest becomes a fire that spreads across the continent. You have my support, Mr. Holmes, whatever it may take," Daisy said.

As the train rattled toward Budapest, we sat silently and took our fill of breakfast. We had little more to say, knowing that the stakes of this game had shifted. War might be on the horizon, but something darker, something far older, lurked beneath the surface.

27

MANIPULATE

Then, in a flurry, a woman entered the carriage and hurried towards our table. I assumed that it was the maid to the Princess, and I was correct. Dark-haired, dressed all in black, long black skirt and heavy knitted woolen shawl covered her from neck to ankle. A small black bonnet, held to her hair by the longest pin, survived the urgency. She arrived at the table as though she was being chased from a funeral by some lost amazonian tribe.

"I'm sorry to have to disturb you, Princess. The baby, he is asleep, but when he wakes, he will be hungry. May I ask the chef to prepare a small bowl of porridge?" She said, panting.

"That's fine Miss Dagian, and get them to add a touch of honey, you know he adores that."

"Thank you, Princess," the maid said, and scurried away at the same speed as she had arrived.

"She's very dedicated. Miss Dagian has accompanied me on all my visits since the birth of my son."

We took our leave of the Princess and returned to the sleeping car. As we entered the carriage, we encountered the car attendant leaving cabin two as we approached our own. He appeared flustered as his shaking hands removed the tab marked 'Robertson.'

"The man left then?" I said.

"I'm not sure if it was a man or a woman," the attendant embarrassedly replied, "I never saw them enter or leave the cabin. Although they must have passed me at some point when they boarded the train."

"I don't understand. I saw you discussing table arrangements last evening with the occupant, did I not?"

"Yes, you did sir. I did not have sight of the occupier. They remained hidden behind the door for the duration of the conversation. They requested to reserve a table close to yours. But at this moment I'm unsure if they even took breakfast. The voice was a whisper and appeared strange when we conversed."

"How so?" asked Holmes.

"It was as if the sound was in my head. So strange that I now find it difficult to assert a male or female

identity to it. I think it could have been either or both."
The attendant put his hand over his mouth in an
attempt to quell the words coming from his lips.

"The next questions are somewhat important, and I
hope you can bring yourself to answer them."

"I will try sir," he said glancing around nervously.

"Which table did the occupant ask to sit at for
breakfast?" said Holmes.

"The table directly to the side of yours."

"I see," Holmes replied.

"Do you think this person disembarked at Munich?"

"It could have been there or earlier at Strasbourg."

"There's no indication?"

"Look for yourself." The attendant opened the cabin
door to its full extent. Inside, everything appeared to
be in its place. The bed remained as it would be found
on boarding, the welcome basket sat in its center. It
was obvious to me that the cabin was not in a state
that showed any sign of occupancy. "I have never seen
the likes of this before. In my experience, no passenger
has ever left the cabin in this condition." His shock
was palpable.

"I agree, it's very unusual indeed. Holmes reached into
his pocket and gave the attendant a coin. "Thank you
for your time," then he turned to me, "Watson, meet
me in my cabin, and we shall discuss our progress,"

Holmes said.

"Certainly, Holmes, I'm glad you find we are making some. I, myself, am uncertain," I admitted, the doubt in my voice, reflecting the mystery of our case.

The attendant stumbled away, still in a state of shock. Holmes returned to his cabin, and as I entered my own, the door swung open. I halted in my stride, standing on the threshold of the room. I peered around the door frame to observe the contents.

I shivered as I caught my reflection in the mirror, which had delivered the three sirens to my side only hours before, and recalled Van Helsing's words "everything has a mirror image, excepting vampires."

Those three mysterious figures, whose appearance most certainly are connected to this unfolding mystery. Still, I could not quite fathom exactly why they had chosen me. But, whatever the reason, I could not bear to look into the glass any longer. I took a bed sheet, unfolded it to its fullest extent and covered the reflection from top to bottom.

After refreshing myself and my clothing, I left my cabin, clicked the lock, and in three steps I was at Holmes's unlatched door. I knocked and waited for a response. There being none, and with some hesitation, I opened the door slowly and moved inside on my tiptoes. Sitting in his chair with his pipe in hand, Holmes had his eyes closed, deep in thought. I waited, Holmes sat so long in deep thought that it seemed to me that he had forgotten my presence, if he had even noted it at all.

"Robertson's cabin, Holmes. What do you make of it? It may be connected to what happened to me last evening, don't you think?"

"I beg you, not at this time, please, Dr. I need to smoke to reset my thoughts. This problem is quite the thing, and I request that you do not disturb me for at least thirty minutes while I allow my thoughts to coalesce." He drew his knees up to his chin and wrapped his arms around his shins to hold them in place. The heels of his shoes hung at the rim of his seat.

This was not a great surprise to me, as I had seen him take such a position several times before, especially when an issue required a plan of action to be thought through. As he sat silently, his cherry wood pipe remained gritted between his teeth while I waited at his desk. A rising thin plume of smoke rose from the smoldering tobacco and wisped against the paneled ceiling. The train rocked and burbled along.

I passed the time by reading the remaining news from the papers, which were still stacked on the desk. Skipping by the births, marriages, and deaths and a notice regarding the serialization of Dr. Conan Doyle's illustrated account of the Great Boar War, I found a small report. The news was of the arrest at the French-Italian border of John Guiappa, an American anarchist who was allegedly on a mission to assassinate the Austrian Emperor. Another article described the strange occurrence at Romford, England, where a young man was found on a train returning from Folkestone without remembering who he was. He could not converse. The solitary clue to the identity was that his only response to questioning was in writing the word 'Robertson.' Before I could consider further the remarkable coincidence of what I had read, Holmes opened his eyes and leaped briskly to his feet.

"Now, tell me more about your happening then, Watson."

"You recall Harker's Journal, the one we received those years ago?

"Of course, what of it, Watson?"

"The encounter between Harker and the three women who visited his chamber. Well, I'm certain that the same three were at my bedside last night. That's why I was late for breakfast earlier."

"You are unmarked?"

"Yes, thanks to this." I pulled Van Helsing's protective charm from under my shirt. The silver glinted in the light as I held it up. Then I remembered the feeling of the woman's fingernails scratching down the flesh of my forearm. I rolled the sleeve to the elbow to reveal the lines.

"Maybe I am marked after all." Three red lines ran

almost parallel from just below the elbow to two inches above the wrist.

"Hmm, let me see."

Holmes prodded the marks, which were evident in their freshness. Tiny beads of blood oozed from the half-healed scratch as he pressed the skin around it.

"Hold out your right hand, Watson, palm down if you will."

I held out my hand, and Holmes glanced at it cursorily.

"Hmm, not self-inflicted. Your fingernails are too wide and blunt for such marks."

"I'm happy you take my word for the event, Holmes," I said with a degree of sarcasm.

"Stranger dreams have rendered similar marks. Dr. I had to allow the facts to speak."

"As you will, Holmes. But what more do you deduct from my experience?"

"We have observed the tactics of the Count on many occasions, have we not?"

"Of course, they have been many and varied, Holmes."

"Then what are your own thoughts on the matter, Dr?"

"Well, maybe an attempt to convert me into one of them, eh?"

"More than that, Watson, a demonstration that he can

manipulate thoughts through apparitions and hypnosis."

"These were more than apparitions, Holmes."

"Take out Van Helsing's charm and remove it from its chain."

I removed the charm and passed it to Holmes. He raised it to the light and turned it with his fingertips through the air, inspecting its form and arrangement.

"Now, your arm and its lines, if you please."

I turned my arm to reveal the marks and held it towards the detective. Holmes turned the charm and laid it at a right angle to the lines on my forearm. He positioned the object on the edge so that three of its points lay directly over the scratch marks. He made an action that drew the sharp points of the metal down my arm. They ran like a train on its tracks.

"You made the marks yourself, Watson. The Count invaded your imagination."

"The event was so real, I find the facts hard to accept." I was stalled in thought with nowhere to go, so I returned to my original subject. "But, what of the cabin, Holmes, and this character Robertson?"

"Likely not the name connected with the true occupant. Think of our breakfast and the passengers sitting closest to our table. Maybe we can narrow the identity of this enigma."

28

SEARCH

The rolling hills of Upper Austria filled the cabin window. The vineyards and forests blended together like a tapestry woven from the paintings of the great French artists Renoir, Degas, and Monet. Holmes paced around the cabin, and we set about recalling the layout of the restaurant car at breakfast. Our task was to confirm our position in relation to the other tables and then identify the passengers at each.

Time marched towards lunch. It was 11 a.m., and we only had two hours before the train made its next stop at Vienna, where I believed we would receive return telegrams from Lestrade and Quincey. Holmes stopped in front of the mirror and momentarily considered his reflection.

"Think, Watson, how many tables were set in the

breakfast car when we entered?"

I attempted to visualize the car's layout and length. It was a long car, two tables wide, spaced evenly down the carriage. An even number would be a good starting point, so I closed my eyes and attempted to form a mental image of the space.

"Somewhere in the region of twelve, I would say."

"Hmm. And how many seats at each?"

"The tables were all set for four, but not all were taken, and not all had a full complement in attendance, some even having none. Considering the number of passengers on the train to be around fifty at maximum, the total would work."

"Let's consider the locations of ourselves and the passengers in proximity."

"We took the second table on the right. Villiers, the journalist, was at the third table on the left. I acknowledged Guinness, sitting alone at the first table as I entered the dining room. A solitary gentleman was at the opposite table to Guinness. The man was directly behind me as we sat. I did not get a good look at him. You must have Holmes?"

"Yes, I did, and for some time. The man was dressed most casually, understated, and far less formal than the rest of us. A light tweed jacket with worn pockets, almost like a gamekeeper's. His breakfast was very particular, one rasher of bacon, two sausages, and four eggs. All were neatly laid out on separate plates. The contents of each plate were methodically eaten, each using its own dedicated and individual set of silverware. I suspect he has an organizational behavioral condition."

"Quite remarkable. Would this man be the one observing us? Doesn't he seem like an acceptable candidate to be touched by this spying stuff?"

"His most excentric behavior had already been noted and catered for by the servers. The man is, therefore, a regular traveler on this train and of no great concern to us, being most conspicuous in these surroundings and not having a need for any particular destination but only of routine."

"I see," I said, rubbing my chin between my forefinger and thumb. "Then there was Green. He was seated beyond the two businessmen at the table directly adjacent to the back of your chair."

"Yes, Mr. Green. His white complexion, pale lips, and dark blue undereye baggage gave away the game, Watson."

"What game do you detect, Holmes?"

"The content of his breakfast," Holmes looked at me as though I had missed the most obvious fact that could be presented on a plate.

"The serving consisted of a small rack of rather burnt toast. Within Green's own reckoning, the butter-coated charcoal would act to soothe the lining of his stomach and engage and reduce its gaseous products all in one."

"You are more than astute. Green has suffered from a rather delicate ailment since the Channel and his visit to the food sellers. Then what of the two businessmen, Holmes?"

"Heading to Bratislava via Budapest. They are equipping a new factory. Messer's Manion and Pontrelli are on a mission to install automatic cork bottling machinery for their employers, Savory and Moore of London. I had the pleasure of overhearing a great deal of their conversation with the server before you had the overdue courtesy of joining me."

"Hum. It was fortunate that I was late then, or you mightn't have gleaned that information."

"As you say, Dr."

Holmes steadied himself. One forearm rested on the window's upper edge, and he gazed out into the distance without focus. His other hand reached down towards his jacket pocket.

"The table directly opposite our own, Watson. Who was there?"

"Why no one, Holmes. I presumed the Princess was heading in that direction before she recognized you and sat with us."

Holmes began pulling the pipe out of his pocket with

his fingertips, gently easing it free. His eyebrows pinched together in sudden concentration. Then, as we were set to think further, a series of panicked raps came at the door, quickly becoming an urgent pounding.

"That sounds ominous," I said.

"Then let them in, man. If that is the case, then we must act swiftly," Holmes urged, emphasizing the need for immediate action.

I opened the door with slight trepidation. In fear of being overwhelmed, I kept the toe of my shoe against the foot of the rear of the door. My head whirled as I considered my own experience with the visions and the fact that we were hunting, for now, an unidentified, and perhaps dangerous, informer in our midst. From our discussion only moments before, I did not have a clear suspect in my mind. Still, Holmes' expression and his grasp of his pipe gave away a clue that I had seen on many occasions at a moment when he had discovered a crucial lead. I opened the door. In the corridor, the attendant stood, mouth agape. A wash of anxiousness mixed with relief covered his face.

"Mr. Holmes...Dr. Watson," The attendant panted. His face blushed at his desperation to find help.

"What is it?"

"It is...Mr. Guinness...something is wrong!" the attendant's sentence shattered by short breaths, deepening the redness of his face.

"Where?"

"In his cabin...he is unconscious...I went to his room to remind him of our approach to Vienna. He had requested that I do so some fifty minutes before arrival."

"Did he provide you with a reason?"

"No, he didn't say why."

We followed the attendant through the passageways to the second sleeping car. When we arrived at the appropriate cabin, the one with 'Guinness' labeled on the halfway open door, another attendant shifted side to side beside the unconscious, or perhaps now dead, man. It was difficult to ascertain immediately what condition Guinness lay in.

Guinness was still sitting in his chair but slumped forward at his desk. His head was on its side and faced us with closed eyes. A small trickle of blood leaked from a small wound at the rear of the head just below the hairline and ran down the nape of his neck to his shirt collar.

"Let me see, I'm a Dr," I roared.

I bent over, my ear as close as possible to Guinness's nose and mouth then listened. The attendants were chatting at speed against one another's nerves, animating their arms in wild circular wheels. The train rattled and swayed with its usual rhythm, causing objects in the cabin to chime against each other. It was as if everything sounded deliberately louder.

"Quiet, please!" I shouted and raised one arm in the air for greater effect.

The attendants stopped whirling their arms, and their discussion quieted. I placed my ear as close as it could be without touching Guinness and listened and listened. I was just about to gather myself to relay the worst when, over the train's rattle, I heard the rasp of a short breath.

"He is still breathing!"

"We can deliver him to the hospital when we arrive in Vienna," the sleeping car attendant said, his voice resonating with relief.

"Move him to bed," I commanded.

"Wait, before you have him repositioned, let me examine the man," said Holmes, his tone severe and urgent, conveying the gravity of the situation.

Before anyone could object, Holmes moved across the cabin beside the folded body. The detective popped his hand over the small wound in the back of Guinness's head and gently felt around it with his fingertips, almost smoothing the flesh beneath.

"Hum, the swelling indicates he has taken a heavy blow."

Holmes bent forward, his eyes squinted as he

examined the wound at close range.

"I see. Now, let's move the poor man to bed."

The attendants positioned themselves on either side of Guinness, and each took hold under the still limp body's armpits. I removed the chair. The injured man grunted loudly as he was manhandled onto the bed. While the attendants were busily heaving the unconscious man onto the bed, I glanced at Holmes, who was in the process of taking a small paper note that must have been trapped beneath Guinness when he had slumped on to the desk. In one quick move, Holmes folded the note in two and placed it carefully into his jacket pocket without the attendants seeing him do it.

"Not much more we can do other than to ensure he is comfortable until we arrive in Vienna and get him appropriate medical assistance, we shall take our leave. Please inform us of this man's condition if it changes at all," I said.

"If he wakes, I would like the opportunity to talk with him. To my cabin, Dr. I have items to discuss before lunch," said Holmes as he hurried from the cabin. We did not speak with Guinness again.

29

ADMIRALTY

We remained quiet as we marched toward Holmes' sleeper cabin, with not a word said between us. On entering the room, I turned and snicked the lock of the door as it drew behind us. Holmes pulled his chair to face more in the direction of the window, then retrieved his pipe and tobacco pouch from his pocket and ignited them without effort. He drew a deep breath and held it for a good time until it was released in a great plume of curling smoke. In a couple more puffs, the whole room filled with the acrid stench of his burning shag.

The smell took me back to our times at Baker Street. Indeed, Holmes was stretched in the chair in his usual form, eyes closed, his face full of contemplation. If we were not confined to this train, it would be easy to imagine we were in the detective's lounge and sitting in front of a great fire.

"What did you find, Holmes? I observed you retrieved evidence from beneath Guinness," I asked.

Holmes took two more puffs before opening his eyes to peer through the cloud of smoke. Through the vapor I caught his lips curling at their ends.

"I examined the point of impact and its wound on the rear of Guinness' head. The mark was made by a closed fist. Judging by the position of the mark, someone standing behind and to the left struck with a heavy hand," Holmes said. He was looking into the distant hills as they trundled across the horizon.

"But how could someone get into the cabin and behind Guinness without him knowing they were there?" I pressed, the mystery thickening more the smoke laden air.

"They were already in the room, invited or not," Holmes said, dismissing the matter as a fact.

"You can tell by examination of the wound?"

"Whoever was responsible swung in a direction from right to left. The split in the flesh opened on the right and pushed across the scalp. The swelling held an additional imprint. I can only surmise the knuckle, together with an object attached to the ring finger, did the damage."

"An object?"

"Yes, leaving the imprint of a double-headed eagle."

"My word, like the rings in our collection? Outstanding Holmes. Then we only need to find the wearer."

"I believe Guinness knew the suspect and had found them already."

Holmes knocked out the tobacco embers into a bowl with three firm strikes. He had brought this frustrating habit from Baker Street; the ornate container was intended for something other than such work. The detective reached out and balanced his pipe on the windowsill, I waited for it to fall, but it held. He reached into his pocket and drew out the paper, a draft telegram note, unfolding it to reveal its content.

"Evidently, the victim was in the process of writing this communication when he was attacked. It is addressed to 'The Gas Company, Southwark, London.' And has the message

MOTH IDENTIFIED. HABITAT AT 1. RETURN RM231. BUDAPEST.

"Well, then, we are no closer. We already knew that Budapest was his destination. Now evidently with a moth of some sort, Holmes."

"My dear Watson, please review the contents again," said Holmes disparagingly thrusting the note in my direction. I stepped forward and reached for it, then reading it to myself considered its content, but still without any great revelation.

"The Gas Company, why on earth would he be writing about a moth to the gas company?"

"A cover for Admiralty House, Watson. An accepted route for British agents to contact the intelligence service. All telegrams addressed in such a manner would be delivered to a small office. In that office, the telegram would be deciphered. But let me ask you, as I don't think this note has much ciphering to it, what are the habits of a moth, Dr?"

"Well, they will fly by night, eh..." My own words struck the back of my head like block of wood. Oh, my word, Holmes, it's a metaphor for Dracula, and his clan!" I exclaimed, the realization hitting me like a bolt of lightning.

"Precisely, Watson. Guinness knew at least one person on this train was running with the Count. I suspect that there may be more than one as he may have unwittingly invited the other to his own carriage."

"The most common companion to Guiness on this journey has been Green, Holmes. I have not witnessed other conversations with any other passenger."

"Yes, your observation tracks mine. I have considered the proximity of the men, but we have not been at their side at all times to be able to confirm what their interactions are about. More importantly, we are left somewhat in the dark, as there have been liaisons between many different passengers and service staff happening that we have not witnessed directly. Although I have my suspicions. Now, what do you pull from the remainder of the message, Watson?"

"Habitat at one. Well, I am stuck."

"What is a habitat other than a place where the 'moth' can be seen at residing in comfort? The number one may indicate a time. The question is then where on this train do passengers gather?" Holmes said, leading me to the answer like a child to a boiled sweet.

"Why, the lounge," I said with a sense of failing achievement, quickly following with, "one, that is the time that lunch is set. An arrangement to meet in the lounge and take lunch together?"

"Perfectly placed, Dr. Then what of the statement, 'Return RM231'?"

"That part I am stumped," I said and ruffled the hair on the back of my head in an up and down sawing motion.

"In all probability the room number of a Hotel. The name of which we are yet to discover."

Holmes glanced at the clock on the desk and leaped to his feet.

"Come we should attend the lounge car and seek to find who Guiness was set to meet," Holmes said, a palpable urgency lay in his voice.

The corridors between the carriages rocked us side to side as we made our way to the lounge car. I braced myself by alternate hands as I walked at pace. I felt again a presence behind, and I turned to see the dark figure darting from the far end of the carriage. We entered the lounge, full of polished mahogany and lit with the soft glow of gas lamps, all muted with a thin haze of cigar smoke, like a gentlemen's club. The murmur of conversation halted. All eyes turned in our direction, some with curiosity, others with suspicion. Then the low buzz of words continued like a smoke-sedated beehive.

At the far end, I saw the Princess seated with a lady whom we had yet to encounter. In front of them, occupying two plush armchairs, were Green, and the journalist Villiers in deep conversation. The two businessmen huddled together around a small glass table filled with glasses of cognac, and were drinking with some abandon. They took it in turn to lean back and guffaw at the other's wit. In a corner, separated from the others, the man and young woman sat and gazed into each other's eyes. The scruffy man, we had noted at breakfast, sat alone in an oversized, winged-back chair with a bottle of red wine for company. There were others that, for the moment, we did not know to be able to identify.

"Most, if not all, the people we observed at breakfast," I said, trying to keep my voice low to avoid drawing more attention to us.

"Let's join Green and the journalist and see where that takes us, shall we?" Holmes suggested. He scanned the room for any sign of the suspects.

30

LOUNGE

We stepped towards the small glass topped, round table holding Green and the journalist. Green, pale, and now rather gaunt, glanced at us and stood unsteadily groping at the top of his chair as the carriage shifted as it rolled over a switch in the track. Villiers also stood, he had no difficulty with his balance.

"Mr. Watson, good to see you. May I introduce you to Frederic Villiers, the renowned war correspondent," said Green.

Villiers stood, a tall and lean figure presumably from years of travel and wore the well-tailored yet weathered suit as he had at breakfast. His grey mustache held behind it an air of quiet intensity about him, a man who had seen the raw edges of war and returned with his soul intact.

"Nice to meet you, Mr. Villiers. I have read your detailed reports and viewed your drawings on many occasions; they are very informative. This is my friend, the great detective Sherlock Holmes."

"Delighted, Mr. Watson...Sherlock Holmes, eh? Well, now, is there a case afoot, detective, as you say?" Villiers blue eyes darted keenly at our faces as he studied our likenesses, pushing their forms into his store of characters for later use.

"Please, let's all be seated." We sat, and Villiers continued, "I, in return, have also read of your exploits, mostly in London over recent times. The Orient Express takes you somewhere or to something of interest?"

"Very likely, Mr. Villiers, it depends on several delicate factors. May I ask what brings you here?"

"A note, detective. A very curious note that I had to act upon."

"May I ask its contents?"

"You may, Mr. Holmes, but only in exchange for details of your business."

"A fair exchange, only to the point that I may have to withhold some information to protect others. I promise that I shall tell you all that I'm able to reveal at this moment. If that is acceptable to you, Mr. Villiers?"

"This is quite interesting, isn't it?" Green's sudden enthusiasm was noticeable, a slight pink tint entering his cheeks, the first sign of any pigment I had seen since our first meeting on the Channel crossing. The tension in the air was thick, each of us waiting for the next revelation.

"Then, Mr. Villiers, what about the note's content?"

"It was a note, detective. A very curious note that I had to act upon. It hinted at something of world-shaking importance about to happen in the area of Budapest. Since I'm associated with reporting on war areas, I presume that a conflict of sorts is about to occur." The mystery of the note's content swirled around, lifting our curiosity.

"There's trouble ahead?" Green asked, his palms smoothed down the top of each leg.

"Usually, when I'm in attendance," said Villiers with a calm demeanor.

"What did the note say exactly, and who was it from?"

"When I say note, it was a telegram, quite cryptic, I would propose. I have it here. I ponder it regularly, so I keep it close."

Villiers reached inside his jacket and pulled out the telegram. He handed it to Holmes, who read it aloud.

"Hmm, it's from the Gas Company," Holmes said. I gave a short huff in surprise. It seemed that Villiers was, without question, involved in this matter in some way."

"Yes, rather a strange origin, but read on if you will."

TWO EAGLES. STRIKE ROYALTY. WAR. BUDAPEST. APRIL LATE.

This cryptic message resembled the handwritten note Holmes found underneath the injured Mr. Guiness. At that moment, when Holmes and our group sat in surprise and thought, I noticed the regal figure of the Princess in heated discussion with the attendant. After a moment of calm, Daisy rose from her seat and left the the lounge, hurrying past us towards the dining car.

"We're almost in Vienna," I said, the anticipation for Holmes's next submission sweeping over me. Would he mention the similarly cryptic message we had in our possession? The suspense was almost unbearable.

"What do you make of the message, detective?" Villiers asked. He leaned forward in his chair and picked up a glass of half-consumed whiskey. "You should have something to wet your throat before you answer." Villiers turned to the bar, swallowed the remaining whiskey in one gulp, raised his glass jubilantly above his head, and called, "Barman, please, get me another and get these gentlemen whatever they want."

The barman raised his eyebrows, came to our table, and took our orders, then returned with a tray of drinks.

"I can let you know of two things that weave from our investigation through the contents of this telegram," Holmes said. "The first is we know of a plot to carry out a destabilizing activity in Budapest in the next few days, which will fit into the timeline as described."

"The rest?" asked Villiers. He had now become particularly interested in our investigation.

"The double-headed eagle."

"What of it? I have seen such in France. It is a symbol that reaches back across the continent hundreds of years."

"We have found examples of the same symbol within ornamentation carried by the disciples, who we suspect are linked to the plot. The likeness has been forged within the head of gold rings."

Holmes reached into his jacket pocket and extracted a bundled handkerchief. He unfurled the cotton to reveal one of the golden rings in the center of his palm. Both Villiers and Green leaned towards the jewelry.

"May I?" asked Villiers.

"Please, do help yourself," replied Holmes, pushing his palm towards the correspondent.

The ring was plucked gently from its resting place and raised into the brightest light before the journalist's eyes. Villiers turned it in all directions, examining each part in great detail.

"The eagles," the correspondent said, "and other markings."

"Here, this may help." Holmes scrabbled in his pocket and pulled out his magnifying eyeglass. Then passed it to Villiers.

"Hmm, inscription, in Latin."

"Hidden by blood," I blurted.

"Quite," Villiers said, passing both items to Green, who set about on his own investigation.

"Have you come across anything resembling this ring on your travels?" Holmes asked. Villiers hesitated and said.

"I may have encountered symbols similar to this when I was in Bulgaria at the end of 1895, covering the war with Serbia. There was a town, Targovishte, if I recall correctly, on the banks of the Vrana River. I was told a legend of a monster who once lived in the town and took the blood of men. A similar double-headed eagle appeared on the Serbian flags. It also reminds me of the symbolism of the Scottish Rite. You have heard of such?"

"The Scottish Rite, Holmes!" I blurted.

"Yes, Watson, it may be a reinforcement of a connection we have already found. Let's move to the remaining parts of the message, Mr. Villiers. What did you take from them, and what was it that brought you to believe its content?"

"We all know there is a widespread feeling that Europe is sitting atop a powder keg of political chess. Each country wants to crown itself as a King. Few historical moments bring so many nations to the same conclusion."

"What is that?" I asked.

"The fact that one strike against another will set the borders of all European nations ablaze. No one will be allowed to sit outside the ring. I have a shiver of war about my flesh, a feeling that something is about to happen. I need to be there when it does. I always do," Villiers said.

Green remained silent, his face dazed. He handed Holmes the ring and magnifying glass and remained silent.

"As for the remaining parts, I suspect that the plot involves an assassination attempt on a member of royalty," Villiers continued before slurping a large portion of his drink.

"We are on the same path," Holmes said.

"Have you spoken with Guinness recently?" I asked Green.

"Not since I passed him good morning at breakfast. Why do you ask?" There was no immediate reaction or anticipation of the news on his face.

"He had an accident. The attendant found him unconscious in his cabin only minutes before we came to the lounge."

"What on earth happened, do you know?"

"Appears he was attacked." Said Holmes.

"Attacked? By someone on this train?"

"Of course, there is no one else, but I think it is more serious than that."

"More serious, how possibly so?"

"I believe that whoever attacked him is part of the grand scheme that we are following. Moreover, there may be more than one amongst us."

Green seemed greatly disturbed. His gaze searched around the remaining passengers in the lounge, seeking some sign that they were somehow the perpetrators. His small, slightly flushed face darkened with emotion.

"This is a terrible thing, Mr. Holmes, a dreadful event. Someone on this train attacked a fellow traveler. We are witnesses to an atrocious situation that is unfolding before our eyes. You seem to have the information to clearly understand where it will lead. Still, we are utterly unable to avert it. Can a human being be placed in a more desperate position?" Green said in a whisper.

"Perhaps not. Whatever we do, we must keep our guards up."

"Who do you think is the principal behind this?" said

Villiers.

"I'm convinced there are more than two conspirators on the train. I must discover them before Budapest."

"Mr. Holmes, I must beg you not to press your investigation to the extent it endangers us all," Green said.

"I am sorry, Mr. Green," said Holmes. "I am accustomed to discovering the mystery. There are others in harm's way. Therefore, I must act."

"You hardly realize the effect of your own action, Mr. Holmes. Good day, gentlemen," Green said and hurried out of the lounge. We would not see him again on the train.

"Well, Mr. Holmes, it seems we are both directed into the unknown," said Villiers.

"Material for your stories and illustrations."

"Budapest is where the story consolidates. This train journey is only a prelude."

The train slowed as it approached its stop in Austria.

31

VIENNA

As we reached the dining car, the train was pulling into the West Bahnhof station. The platform, stretching into the distance, was a hive of activity, filled with uniformed porters, travelers, luggage, and station officials. It was the most chaotic of arrivals, the noise punctuated by shouting and whistles. This straightforward station, devoid of the opulence of others, was a whirlwind of activity, a clear sign of the disarray we were about to step into.

We took our place at the same table as we had during breakfast. We intended to note who returned to their original place and identify others we had yet to thoroughly examine. The passenger, we shall call the gamekeeper, due to his dress, was sitting at his usual place. This time, his lunch ingredients were spread on different plates so they would not contact each other.

"There will be quite a delay, Holmes. The train will need to be overturned. I read about it before we departed," I said.

"You have me there for once, Watson. Tell me what that operation entails. At the same time, keep an eye on those who are boarding and, of course, departing. This is the last stop before Budapest. I anticipate we will receive return messages from Lestrade and Quincey. Our role here is to observe and gather information, not to intervene unless absolutely necessary," Holmes explained.

"It means the engine will be replaced by another at the opposite end."

"How quaint. Now, please, let's observe the situation."

A flurry of activity occurred as a stretcher carrying poor Guinness was carried out onto the platform. Waiting passengers parted their ranks to allow the convoy of attendants to pass. Guinness had not regained his senses and had slipped further into unconsciousness. We heard later in the week that he was to die in hospital before the next day. I was confident that the blow alone could not have been the reason for his demise. I was proven correct only after a detailed examination of the body by the authorities in Austria.

The dining car attendant appeared at our side and

handed two telegrams to Holmes. The first response, from Lestrade, was of utmost importance. This message confirmed our suspicions about Boschetti's activities and the potential for violence. It was a crucial piece of information for our investigation, Holmes explained, his tone serious and focused.

BOCHETTI HIDING MONTHS. NETWORK ESTABLISHED. VIOLENCE IMMINENT. CONTACT INSPECTOR KOVÁCS.

LESTRADE

"The answer seems to be clear, Holmes. I do not have any confusion about its meaning."

"And neither will anyone who has had sight of it. This anarchist Boschetti will be the connection between us and Dracula, Watson. I hope that this message has fallen into the appropriate hands. And importantly, the Count will already have realized our aim before we arrive in Budapest. We both know that Dracula is a formidable adversary, and we must continue to be cautious in our dealings with him," Holmes warned, his voice hanging with impending danger, heightening the suspense.

"But you lead him to us, Holmes?"

"No, Watson, we lead Boschetti to him. Dracula will call the anarchist to his side, and we will be in his tracks, not his path."

"As you say, one way or the other, it sounds rather like a trap to me, and I don't want to be the mouse."

"And so, we will not be."

"My good man, your tactics are somewhat beyond my grasp, and as always, I have to trust in your judgment as you have rarely been wrong."

"There have been times, but now for the next reply."

It was the response from Quincey. I waited in anticipation for the news that he was safe and well. Holmes opened the note and read:

LONG WALK WITH PRINCE

QUINCEY

"Is that it? He walks the pup, and that is his news! Good gracious, Holmes."

"There is more news there than you can imagine, Dr. Now I need to set out the appropriate replies."

Holmes thought momentarily while I peered against the window, seeking anyone boarding the train on its last leg. The detective took two pieces of paper from his pocket and scribbled simple messages onto both with a pencil, each word having a very specific purpose in our investigation.

"Return this message to Lestrade."

PLAYERS KNOWN. HEAD SOUGHT

"Return this to Quincey."

TAKE A BONE

"Take a bone? What on earth is this exchange about?"

"Send the messages as written, and all will be clear."

I hurried back to the lounge, found the concierge, and placed both telegrams to be sent. I returned with a newspaper, a local Hungarian news. I glanced at the front-page headline and picked out the word BOSCHETTI, from the rest '*AZ ANARCHISTA BOSCETTI A BUDAPESTI UTCÁKBAN*'. This could not be of any coincidence. We just required someone on this train who is able and willing to translate it for us.

Returning to the Dining Car, I glanced from the window to observe the activity on the platform. In the midst of the jostling crowd, I saw again the shape of the dark figure, this time it was weaving against the tide of people wandering along the platform. The unidentified person appeared to take a final glance at the train over their shoulder and then disappeared into the melee.

Holmes was seated and deep in thought.

"Holmes, the telegraphs are sent. But look, in a local newspaper, there is a headline that obviously involves Boschetti. It's in Hungarian."

32

LUNCH

A voice crackled from the table behind Holmes.

"I can help translate."

It was the 'gamekeeper,' a man we had never spoken to before. He was a mysterious figure, often seen in the dining car but never interacting with the passengers. To us, he was a man of strange habits and unknown purpose. The man pushed the four plates in front of him to the center of the table and walked over to our table. He stood beside Holmes and reached his hand out in greeting.

"I am Gyula Lengyel. I hear you need to translate Hungarian. I can do it for you. It is not an easy language. I overheard your conversation and thought

I could be of assistance," he explained.

"Mr. Lengyel, I am very pleased to meet you. Let me introduce you to my good friend, Dr. John Watson," said Holmes.

"Yes, I know you both well. Your reputation precedes you, Mr. Holmes, the famous detective?"

"I hear my feats are the talk of fashionable society, please take a seat with us, Mr. Lengyel."

"I will sit with you as long as you don't take food until I've completed my business with you. I cannot bear how people mix up their meals as they eat. I find it rather, as you say, unsavory, like pig swill," Lengyel said, his eyes darting around the room to record if anyone close to us was breaking his rule. His aversion to food mixing was a quirk that many found peculiar, but it was a rule he seemed to strictly adhere to.

"As you wish, Mr. Lengyel. We understand. You are Hungarian, then?" asked Holmes.

"A mix, you might say, a mongrel. I travel all over Europe using this vehicle. It's almost my home. I'm well-known by the crew, who take good care of me. Mind you, I pay them enough."

"Why is it that you choose to reside on the Express?" I asked.

"It's a long story."

"Give us a short version, then," I said, and Lengyel

laughed. He sounded like a large bullfrog.

"The short story is, I do it so I don't get caught up in the politics of nationalism, which flows through Europe like a river. It's a recipe for disaster, but we are all too proud to realize it. That's nationalism, I suppose. Here, on the Express, I can be anywhere in Europe in a day or so. I might even go to America one day, as others have already done. Now, what is it that you wish me to translate?"

"We have a newspaper article here; see," I placed the newspaper in front of Lengyel:

AZ ANARCHISTA BOSCETTI A BUDAPESTI UTCÁKBAN.

"Ah, the anarchists. Let me see," he scanned the text and began to read, carefully running his index finger under each line of text.

"The Anarchist Boschetti in the Streets of Budapest.

"Authorities suspect Boschetti has been hiding in Budapest since August. He is suspected of using a network of underground operatives to evade detection. His re-emergence brings with it a threat to all citizens and signals the potential for violence.

"The police have launched a full-scale operation, meticulously combing through the streets of the Castle District and monitoring key transportation routes. Inspector Kovács has confirmed that additional patrols have been deployed to the city's train stations and river docks, leaving no potential escape route unchecked. The city is on high alert, and every corner is under intense scrutiny.

"Authorities have also warned government officials and nobility to heighten their security precautions, particularly in light of Boschetti's known penchant for targeting figures of authority and royalty. The streets around Buda Castle have seen an increased police presence, and local citizens are urged to remain vigilant.

"The Hungarian government has responded quickly, with Minister of the Interior Count István Tisza condemning the rise of anarchist activity and vowing to cooperate with international law enforcement to bring Boschetti to justice. In a statement to the press, Tisza declared that Hungary would not be a breeding ground for foreign radicals. We stand united in the fight against those who seek to undermine order and sow terror."

"Hmm, it sounds like there may be some trouble ahead."

As Lengyel paused, the locomotive shuddered, rocking the Dining Car backward and forward. Whistles screamed at passengers remaining on the platform to complete their boarding. Steam pushed its way at ankle level along the terminal.

"Thank you, this is very useful. Are you staying in Budapest?" said Holmes.

"Only for a few days."

"With family?"

"I have none. I will stay at the Hotel Hungaria, I have a suite there. They know me well, too. If that is all, gentlemen, I will bid you a good remainder of the journey."

"Thank you again. We may bump into you in the city," I said. Lengyel smiled and returned to his table. He signaled to the attendant, who brought fresh plates to his table.

"Rather fortunate, don't you think, Holmes," he did not respond as he was distracted by a figure scurrying towards us. He leaped out of his chair, and upon seeing our visitor, I followed.

"Princess, are you alright?" Holmes said.

"Why, Mr. Holmes and Dr, I am in such a tangle," Daisy said, her breath short and face flushed.

"Please take a chair. And tell us in your own time whatever the issue is." Holmes drew a chair, and Daisy took it, and we returned to ours. Holmes gestured to the attendant, who had just returned to his station, to bring a glass of water.

"Well, you would not believe it. It's Miss Dagian. She departed without a word. Left all her belongings and jumped from the train at this very stop.

"There was no reason?" I said.

"There is always a reason," Holmes replied. "Do you have the belongings that she abandoned?"

"Why, yes. The attendant has all of her luggage in safekeeping."

"What about the care of your child?" I asked.

"The concierge managed to recruit one of the station staff during our stop as a temporary replacement until I reach Budapest. There, I will have to recruit another. Such a task, I will be late for Constantinople, no doubt."

"The belongings, Princes, can I view them?"

"Of course, ask the sleeper car attendant in the second carriage. He has them stowed. Do you think you will find a reason for her departure?"

"It's unlikely, but there may be a clue to wider activities. Watson, make your way to the attendant and ask the case to be delivered to my cabin, then join me there. We have less than four hours to ready ourselves for the encounter."

Holmes took the rear of Daisy's chair and allowed her to remove herself from our table. She made her way across the aisle to the table opposite and seated herself.

"Your table from yesterday?" asked Holmes.

"Yes, it was arranged as soon as we boarded. A delightful coincidence to be seated as close to you as we were, don't you think?"

"Absolutely, Princess. It has been a pleasure to be able to re-acquaint myself with this journey. If you require our assistance while in Budapest, please contact the Hotel Hungaria, as that will be our base," he said.

"I hope your encounter with the forces which plot against us all will be a success. Thank you, and be well, Mr. Sherlock Holmes."

I, in turn, scurried through the passageways to find the attendant and the baggage left by Miss Dagian. After completing my task, I returned to our sleeping car. As I passed the cabin formerly occupied by the unseen 'Robertson,' I noted the door was slightly open. I heard a ruffling of paper. There was no name tag on the door, so I slowly put my head through the crack. That's the last I remember.

33

BAGGAGE

I awoke with a start to the sprinkling of cold water across my face like ice on a winter shower. Staring at the ceiling, I was on my back, and my head throbbed. I could make out a fuzzy form standing over me. I put my hand behind the back of my head and felt a sharp pain as I put too much pressure on a large lump.

"Dr., are you alright?" The familiar voice said.

"What happened?" I groaned.

"You were hit on the head, Dr." said the voice I now recognized as the sleeper car attendant.

Then, another figure entered the cabin.

"Watson! What on earth, are you alright?" Holmes' voice was filled with genuine concern.

"Yes, just a bit groggy, old man. It must have been a heavy wallop. Help me sit."

"I was on my way to deliver the baggage as requested. The case was used by Miss Dagian and left in her cabin."

"Put it in my room, lad. I'll take care of Dr. Watson here."

Holmes helped me onto the chair, and the attendant moved the baggage from the corridor to Holmes' cabin. Other than a slight ringing in one ear, I was fine. I regained my vision and could see that the room had been ransacked. Papers had been strewn across the room, drawers opened, and the bed ransacked. I placed my handkerchief onto the lump.

"I heard someone in here, so I popped my head in."

"And someone popped your head. You really must be more cautious, Watson. Let me take a look at this bump."

I leaned forward and removed the handkerchief, which had a small dot of blood on it. Holmes examined the wound without pressing it as much as he had done with Guinness.

"Hmm, it is the same, Watson. A mark carrying the imprint of the double-headed eagle. The connection is made."

"Who could have done this, Holmes?"

"I must say, at the moment, I am at a loss to pinpoint the subject. Now, let's find what the intruder was looking for, shall we?"

"What if it's already taken?"

"Then our task is to discover what is missing, and quickly," Holmes responded, his tone emphasizing the urgency, "we must also search the baggage left behind by Miss Dagian."

"The room was empty when the person occupying Robertson's cabin vacated it without a trace and disappeared. The room was left in its original state. Nothing seemed to have been used or moved. What could possibly be the reason to disassemble the cabin like this?"

"Someone thought differently."

We searched the cabin from top to bottom. We could find nothing out of the ordinary until Holmes closed the sliding door to the wardrobe. There, a small label, similar to the ones used to mark the cabin door with the identity of the occupant. Holmes lifted it from its position and held it up to his face, a sense of relief in his eyes.

"What does it say, Holmes?"

"Dagian," he replied, "to the baggage."

Once back inside Holmes' cabin, we took the sturdy canvas case, wrapped and secured by thick leather straps and held by thick brass clasps. A small metal nameplate identifying Dagian was attached to its side. There was no lock, and the bag opened without needing Holmes' special lock-picking skills.

Inside, the contents were well organized into several compartments. We took turns pulling everything clear and laying the items onto the bed for further examination. There were general items one would expect a maid to carry: ironing tools, fabric brushes, safety pins, and jewelry-cleaning cloths. Then, there was personal clothing: nightgowns, an apron, slippers, soap, and a hairbrush, with long strands of dark hair attached.

Holmes reached into the internal side pockets and pulled out a handful of papers, including a luggage receipt, employment contract, wardrobe and outfit plans. He rifled through them, finding nothing of interest until uncovering a folded note.

"Here, we have it."

"What, Holmes?"

"An address in Budapest; why would the maid have an address in Budapest if she was traveling to Constantinople with the Princess."

"A conundrum, Holmes. Do you think she will be traveling there now?"

"That is likely, and she even might be ahead of us."

"How could that be possible?"

"As you said, when we arrived in Vienna, the engine of the Express had to be overturned, which caused a delay in our onward journey. Miss Dagian could have left the train and boarded a direct service while we were still taking lunch."

"Then what of the address, Holmes?"

"Podmaniczky Utca 45, Budapest."

34

BUDAPEST

The train reached Budapest's Keleti Station a little past 5 p.m. The gaslights lining the platform flickered in the twilight, darkened by the thickening fog as the Orient Express hissed its final breath. Fingers of steam curled from the engine and clawed at the platform.

"A carriage is waiting to take you to the Hungaria, Mr. Holmes," the sleeping car attendant said as our feet hit the platform. A pointed hand directed us to the transportation service provided by the Hotel, which would deliver us directly to the Hungaria's door.

"Your cases will be taken from the baggage car and delivered separately; don't worry, they won't get lost," the attendant said.

"Thank you," said Holmes and hurried towards the attendant. I reached into my pocket, pulled a banknote from my wallet, and slapped it into the attendant's hand. I ran to catch Holmes, who was five steps distant.

"Keep your wits about you, Watson. No time for us to be dallying. We are not left alone in this city. The danger is all around, and we must act," Holmes urged, his voice carrying a sense of urgency.

"I'm with you, Holmes. The Hotel is on the same street as the station, so it should not take over ten minutes."

I followed Holmes as he hurried through a sea of strangers, our footsteps echoing against the station's marble floor. I glanced over my shoulder, half-expecting to glimpse some lurking anarchist hiding amongst the flow of weary travelers. Nothing met my gaze but the throngs of locals and international visitors arriving from Vienna, Prague, and further afield.

A fiacre waited for us on the cobblestone street outside the façade of this recently opened station. Horse-drawn carriages and electric streetcars filled the square beyond. The sound of hooves clattering against the stone streets blended with the hum of the electric motors.

Holmes's sharp, hawkish gaze swept the dimly lit square before us. His face seemed to have an etched gauntness about it. We both knew that somewhere, hidden in the city's folds, Dracula was waiting. The Count was aware that we had arrived, and more likely, he watched every move.

Our carriage driver was a hunched figure wrapped in a heavy coat, his face obscured by the shadow of his hat. Holmes gave him a quick, almost imperceptible nod, and we climbed aboard. The horses set off at a brisk pace down the broad avenue of Rákóczi Ut.

The city passed us in a blur of grand façades and rising smoke from gas-lit lampposts, but there was little comfort in the evening's elegance. A fog was thickening and bringing with it a deep sense of foreboding. I found my hand instinctively resting on the revolver's handle tucked in my coat pocket. Every shadow, every passerby, seemed to harbor menace. The looming danger, Dracula's gaze, cold as the grave, fixed upon us.

The streets became suddenly quieter. Holmes had spoken little since we boarded, his brow furrowed in thought, his eyes occasionally darting toward the darkened alleyways we passed as though expecting an ambush at any moment.

"Dracula's reach is long, Watson," Holmes murmured, almost to himself. "His agents will be scattered like shadows in every dark corner of this city."

I glanced nervously in all directions. The yellow, thick fog was starting to snuff out the light from the gaslights lining the street, which brought chilling memories of our encounters with Dracula in London. I sensed unseen eyes following our every movement.

The Count's influence saturated the air like the fog, which gathered density every second.

We arrived at the Hotel Hungaria. The warm glow of the luxurious entrance welcomed us as our carriage came to a halt. We disembarked, gave the driver a coin, and entered the lobby. We were met by a soft murmur of guests, who turned without halting their chatter to examine the new guests.

"There is a heaviness, Holmes."

"Yes, they all sense danger. It's an instinct we all have. We are studying, my good man. Keep going, and..."

My eyes were drawn immediately to Holmes. He had stopped mid-step, his posture rigid, his eyes locked in concentration and recognition onto a small figure across the room. There, in the shadows, was a girl. The Greek girl, our contact I suspected. Her dark eyes shimmered beneath the glow of chandeliers.

"Elena," Holmes murmured and turned to me.

"She is in danger here. We are too exposed."

Before I could react, Elena swept across the lobby and was upon us.

"They're onto us," she hissed, her voice barely above a whisper. "Boschetti's men are close by. And..." Elena paused, her dark eyes narrowing. "He is near. Dracula himself."

Holmes' expression darkened, and his brows furrowed

with a deep intensity.

"You should not have come here, Elena. It puts you at great risk."

She shook her head vehemently.

"We're running out of time. We must act quickly, or the anarchist's trap will surround us. The need for quick action is dire," Elena emphasized, her voice filled with urgency.

"As I said, Holmes."

Holmes nodded gravely, then turned to me.

"Watson, go to the desk, retrieve our keys, and then we must retreat to our room. There is more at play here than we had anticipated."

I went to the lobby desk. The clerk looked up and smiled with uncomfortable ease.

"Can I help you, sir?"

"Yes. We have a room."

"Your name, please?"

"It should be reserved in the name of Watson," I said. The clerk shuffled through a stack of organized scraps of paper.

"Ah, yes. Dr. Watson and Sherlock Holmes. You have a suite on the fifth floor. I will need your passports and travel documents, please."

I handed the required paperwork over the counter and

received the keys to room 503.

"The elevator is to your right. Have a great stay, and let me know if you need anything. My name is Gregor." I thanked Gregor, and he returned a slick smile as I rejoined Holmes and Elena in the lobby.

"Take the stairs, not the elevator," Holmes said.

I followed Holmes and the girl to the grand staircase, keeping my hand on the pistol's grip as it swung in my jacket pocket. The thick carpet muffled our steps but did little to quiet my heart's racing.

The climb up five floors took our breaths before we reached the door to our suite. Holmes paused, his hand lingering on the key inserted into the lock. He turned to Elena, his voice a whisper. "Do you trust this place?"

She hesitated for the briefest of moments, then nodded. "For now, it is safe. But perhaps, not for long."

With a single, swift motion, Holmes opened the door, and we stepped inside. The room was spacious and elegantly appointed, with velvet drapes and polished wood, but it felt like a prison. Even here, within the sanctuary of the Hotel Hungaria, I knew we were not beyond the reach of the Count's dark influence.

Holmes strode to the window, peering out into the darkness which had closed around us. I saw the tension in his shoulders, the weight of the invisible eyes watching us from the shadows of Budapest.

"Watson, I can now introduce you to Elena Laskaris. You have knowledge of her through the case of her brother's murder."

"Yes, the case of the Greek interpreter had an unfortunate outcome, but it's nice to meet you and have your assistance here."

"It's the least I could offer, Mr. Holmes has advised me on several, shall we say, delicate matters."

"Quite so," I replied, keeping my thoughts and questions regarding the involvement of Elena in the revenge deaths of the perpetrators in Budapest some time ago to myself.

As I looked to the window, seeing nothing but darkness beyond, I could feel the inescapable presence of something malevolent lurking just out of sight. Dracula was watching, and I knew he would not wait long for the strike.

Despite the growing fog, the silhouette of Castle Hill loomed in the distance, dark and oppressive. Holmes's eyes darted briefly toward it, and I followed his gaze toward Elena.

"Boschetti, the anarchist, has been conscripted to do the Count's bidding. We must assume that he will act against us before we can properly plan our move," Holmes said

"The air, Watson," he whispered. "Can you not feel it?"

I did. The air was thick and oppressive as if drawn into some unseen maw. My breath came shallow. I moved to the window, peering through the drapes, and there, just beyond the glass, was a figure, pale and motionless, the monster's eyes burning like red embers.

It was Dracula.

He did not move, yet I felt his presence wrap itself around my throat, tightening. Holmes moved to my side, his jaw set, his eyes sharp as steel.

"He watches Watson, but he cannot enter. Not yet."

I let the curtain fall, my hand trembling.

"What do we do, Holmes?"

"We wait, Watson," Holmes replied.

"For what?" I asked.

"Dracula knows every step we take. We must think and plan our moves carefully. There are others he controls, so his reach is not limited to the twilight hours, and they will not hesitate to come for us."

"There is no safe place or time of day," Elena said.

I drew the curtains to be fully closed. Even so, I felt the dark city of Budapest wrap itself around us like a shroud. And somewhere, just beyond the walls of this Hotel, Dracula waited.

"Waiting until dawn has no benefit; we have to act now. Elena, where will we meet your contacts to the underworld?"

"It is an Inn, the Red Frog. It's in District One, over the river from here. There will be men who will know more than we do."

"It sounds like we are placing ourselves in greater danger than we should, Holmes," I said.

"We have to act fast, Watson. Dracula and his cohort expect us to confine our actions to this room for tonight. It is now we have to use any opportunity to slip through their net," the girl urged, and I knew she was right, but I didn't like the idea of it.

"Quite so, Elena. We shall use the service entrance to work our way into the night unobserved," Holmes said. "But first we must arm ourselves."

"I do not need anything apart from my knife," Elena said, drawing a long straight blade from its sheath at her side.

"It will require a preparation." I said and opened my bag. I removed a jar of holy water.

"Water?"

"Holy Water, our weapons and bullets all require to be coated in this, so we are able to injure our opponents."

Elena said nothing but held her knife ready to receive

its armor. We prepared and gathered all our tools. Prepared for whatever we may encounter we headed out of the Hotel with the hope that we would not be followed.

35

RED FROG

We used the Chain Bridge to cross over the calm expanse of the Danube below. The air was damp with the chill of April as the fog hung along the streets. It was a little past ten o'clock when we made our way down the narrow, winding streets of Buda and into District I. Our destination lurked in the dark shadows of Castle Hill.

"What can you tell me of the Red Frog?" Holmes asked Elena as we walked.

"Other than it's a den of vice and villainy, full of dangerous and desperate men, what is there to know?" she answered, a small smile forming.

"Tell me, how did you come to know of it?"

"When I became desperate, I was led to this place. It was my time of depression when I was tracking down that pair of murderous thieves after they had fled

London. I was determined to take my vengeance, and this was where I found all the information I needed. It is greater than that, though; it is the place I come to hide from prying inquiries."

"Then it proved to be most valuable to your aims."

"Yes, but I must warn you, Sherlock, it is not a place for reputable gentlemen like yourselves."

Then I caught sight of the Inn. It was nestled against the castle hill like some ancient parasite. It exuded an aura of danger, a place where the unwary could easily fall prey. Yet here we were, led by Elena, our mysterious ally, whose knowledge of the city's underworld would soon become invaluable.

The streets were deserted except for a few lurking shadows and stray dogs. The dogs remained quiet, which was a good sign. Watchouts peered at us from alleyways and corners as we passed. Holmes walked a step ahead of us, his tall, lean figure cutting a striking silhouette against the night. His keen eyes flicked over the rooftops and darkened windows with suspicion. The collar of his coat was turned up against the night air, and his features, usually so controlled, were tight with tension.

"You're certain of this place, Elena?" I asked.

"Yes, Dr. Watson," she replied, her voice low, barely above a whisper. "This is where we will find the men you seek. But be careful. They do not take kindly to questions and even less to outsiders."

"Then let us not waste any more time."

The Inn loomed ahead, its dilapidated facade barely distinguishable from the hills surrounding stonework. A dim amber light glowed faintly through the grime-encrusted windows, casting a sickly hue onto the cobblestones at its threshold. From inside came the low murmur of voices, punctuated by occasional bursts of coarse laughter.

A stench of sour ale and sweat hit us immediately as we entered the Inn. The flickering light of an oil lamp struggled to hold back the thick shadows that clung to every corner of the room, and the patrons, hardened men of dubious character, cast hostile glances as we passed.

Holmes moved to an empty table at the far end of the room and sat with his back to the wall. Elena and I followed, the weight of unseen eyes bearing on us. It was only a short time before our entrance drew the attention we sought.

A hulking figure rose from a table closer to the bar, his heavy boots thudding on the floor as he approached. His face was a mess of scars and broken teeth, his nose twisted from more than one brawl. He was a walking embodiment of danger, a man not to be trifled with. He wore a long, threadbare coat that reeked of damp wool and tobacco.

"This is Kerekes. He is most dangerous," Elena whispered between us.

SHERLOCK & DRACULA: THE GREAT WAR

"I know her, but who are you?" the man growled, his voice thick with malice. "You might have made a mistake coming here."

Holmes gave the man a slow, deliberate look, the faintest smile curling at the corner of his lips. "Ah, I had hoped you'd find me. Saves me the trouble of asking for you."

The brute's eyes narrowed. "Do you know me? What do you want?"

"I am told you are called Kerekes. My name id Holmes. I only want to talk."

"We don't deal in talk. We deal in business, and you're bad for business right now." The man snorted. Wisps of saliva flew from his mouth and hung from his tangle of thick, black beard.

"I assure you," Holmes said, calm but sharp as a knife, "I have no interest in your sordid little enterprises. I am, however, interested in Boschetti and his movements. I know he's been working closely with men like you who frequent this establishment. And I believe you know exactly what I'm talking about."

The man's face darkened, his lip curling into a snarl. "You think you can waltz here, ask questions, and walk out alive? You've got some nerve."

Holmes leaned forward, his eyes glittering with cold calculation. "If you want to threaten me, do so. But know this: if you harm me or my friends here, the entire network of anarchists under Boschetti will fall. And that includes you. Every deal you've made, every coin you've earned, will be lost. Now, I offer you a choice: help us, and I may be able to protect you when the time comes. Refuse, and you'll find yourself at the mercy of men far more dangerous than myself."

The room seemed to hold its breath. The man stood frozen for a moment, his thick fingers twitching near the knife's hilt at his belt. Then, with a growl, he slumped back into the chair across from us.

"You're mad to go after Boschetti," he muttered, though the threat had drained from his voice. "He's not the one you should be worrying about."

"And who should I be worrying about?" Holmes asked, his tone betraying nothing.

Kerekes glanced around the room, lowering his voice as if the walls themselves had ears. "They say Boschetti's have been meeting in secret at a location in Ferencváros, near the docks, and working with someone, something not human, only... rumors."

"Rumors of what?" I asked, though my heart already dreaded the answer.

The man leaned forward, his face pale, his eyes darting nervously. "Graves. They're being robbed. All over Europe. Bodies, taken. And they say it's Dracula, that he's raising an army."

The man's expression grew grave. "They say the Count

is using a power older than even himself, older than anything we know. IZ is the spirit which controls the shadows, the souls of the dead. Dracula's using the power to raise his army. He's not just creating more of his own likeness. He's calling forth something else by ritual, something worse."

Elena's voice broke the tense silence. "Where is the ritual being held?"

The man hesitated, clearly torn between fear of betrayal and hope of survival. He glanced toward the door, then back to us, his voice dropping to a near whisper.

"There's a chapel. Beneath the labyrinth, deep in the rock. It's old, older than the castle itself. That's where they'll do it. I don't know when, but it's soon."

Holmes stood abruptly, his long frame casting a shadow over the table. "Thank you, Kerekes. You've been most helpful."

Kerekes sneered, but his fear stuck in his throat. "You think interfering will get you anywhere, Mr. Holmes? Do you think you can stop what's coming? IZ is power beyond your understanding. Even Dracula can't control it."

Holmes paused, his eyes hard as steel. "Perhaps. But I intend to try." He remained still, his sharp eyes locked on Kerekes. "The creatures," he pressed. "Are they any more than legend?"

At that moment, the door to the tavern creaked open, and a chill gust of wind swept in, causing the flames of the nearby candles to flicker wildly.

"You shall find," Kerekes, said softly.

With that, Holmes turned on his heel and strode toward the door, we followed behind. As we stepped back into the cold, foggy air, I couldn't shake the feeling that we were walking into a trap set by forces far darker than anything we had faced before.

"Holmes," I said quietly, "do you truly believe we can stop this?"

Holmes's eyes betrayed the weight of the challenge before us.

"We must, Watson. Dracula is not just gathering an army; he's seeking to enslave the dead. This power they call IZ may provide him with the means to succeed. If cannot sit back and do nothing."

As we left the Red Frog Tavern, we made our way into the night and returned within minutes to the Hungaria. I could not help but feel a heavy weight of dread upon my heart. The labyrinths awaited, and with them, the answers we sought, but perhaps something far darker than any of us had anticipated.

36

HUNGARIA

We returned to the Hotel before the clocks struck one and climbed the stairs to our room. Holmes placed his ear to the door before entering the key into the lock. He turned it with a gentle touch. A slight click told us that its work was done.

"With me," he whispered and placed the full weight of his shoulder onto the door.

With a twist of the handle, the door flew to its widest as we all piled into the room. The space was empty, and the suite was just as we had left. The dark velvet curtains were drawn tight, and the only sound was a distant hum of the Budapest night.

"What is this? A note," I said and lifted an envelope from under my shoe.

The cream letter was composed on Hotel stationary and had Holmes' name printed neatly on its front. I handed the correspondence to him. As was his usual want, Holmes took the envelope and turned it between his fingers, revolving it in front of the flickering flames as he stood by the hearth and concentrated his thought.

"What is it?" Elena asked.

"A message from someone who has an official capacity. The writing is neat and carried by a steady hand. The seal has not been tampered with. I believe this may be information delivered by Inspector Kovács," Holmes replied.

He opened the envelope, drew out a folded piece of paper, and unfurled it with the care of a surgeon. Holmes nodded, his sharp features illuminated by the faint glow of the fire.

"Indeed, it is from Kovács. It is related to Guinness. He died soon after his delivery to the hospital."

"How, it was only a bump on the head, Holmes?" I said, somewhat stunned.

"It was not the blow to his head, though severe, that ended his life."

I felt a chill as I recalled the sight of Mr. Guinness when we had discovered him in his cabin, his body slumped over his writing desk. But he was still alive and breathing when we left him.

"Then what did?" I asked.

"The doctor's findings are clear. It was not the outward violence that killed him, but rather a precise internal wound. His heart was punctured by a long, thin instrument, something sharp, something deliberate."

"An instrument of murder," I muttered.

"Precisely, Watson. And not just any weapon. This was no knife, no common tool of death. It was an instrument of surgical precision, designed to pierce the heart while leaving little evidence of its passage. And that leads us to our culprit."

"Who do you have in mind, Holmes?"

"Recall Miss Dagian," Holmes said, pacing around the room.

"Princess Daisy's maid?"

"Yes, Watson," Holmes stopped pacing, "Miss Dagian, who vanished from the train as it stopped in Vienna. It all fits. What we witnessed on the train was no random act of violence. This was planned."

"The weapon, though, Holmes?"

"Her hat, Watson. Think."

"The pin, Holmes...The long, thin pin," I stuttered.

"Precisely, my good man. Long, sharp, and strong enough to pass into the lower rib cage of Guinness while he was incapacitated and pierce his heart."

"The loss of blood would have been slow and internal. No one noticed the puncture. Poor man," I said.

"But why was this man Guinness the target?" Elena asked.

"He was in the process of informing London of what he had found on the train. He was an agent of British Intelligence. Dagian, or one of her associates, had found him out."

"There was another on that train?"

"I have my suspicions. And we will find confirmation soon."

Sitting in a high-backed chair by the window, Elena stared into the flickering fire. Her hands folded neatly in her lap betrayed no tremor, yet there was a tension about her, as though she too sensed that the unseen forces had drawn closer.

Holmes crossed to the window and peered between a gap in the curtains into the darkened streets below.

"Miss Dagian has been no ordinary maid, Watson. She has used her position to travel and spy on all the leaders of Europe. Acting as the Princess' maid she has discovered and then supplied sensitive information to these dark and dangerous forces. She is in league with the anarchists and may, therefore, also be in Dracula's service," said Holmes.

I stood by the desk, my mind still clouded with the strange terror that had come upon us at the Red Frog, the whispered rumors of Dracula, of IZ, of dark rituals beneath the labyrinth. Then I thought more of Dagian.

"The address, Holmes!" I exclaimed, "The address we found in Robertson's room is Podmanicky Ut 45."

"Podmanicky?" Elena said. "I think that is the street of the new Grand Lodge."

"That's where she is hiding, Holmes?"

"The anarchists, the blended Freemasonry, the undead, and the shadowy power of IZ are all connected. We are no longer dealing with isolated incidents. The attack on Mr. Guinness was part of something much larger, a conspiracy stretching across Europe, threatening not only us but the very fabric of society."

I felt my blood run cold. "And now we are drawn into its web."

Holmes nodded. "Indeed. We are running out of time, Watson. The labyrinths beneath Castle Hill, those ancient tunnels. It is where the key is held. It is there that the anarchists are gathering, and it is there that Dracula may be preparing his army."

Elena shifted slightly in her chair, her dark eyes unmoving from the fire and gleaming with determination. "We must go there, to the labyrinths. We must stop whatever they are planning before it is too late."

Holmes looked at her for a long moment, then nodded.

"Yes, Elena. But we must be cautious. The labyrinth is not merely a place of stone and darkness. It is a living thing, a place that has swallowed men whole. And now, it is possible that it is crawling with the undead."

I could not help but shudder at his words. The idea of descending into those ancient tunnels, with the thought of Dracula's minions lurking in the shadows, filled me with a dread I had experienced twice before. And yet, I knew we had no choice.

"Then when do we go?" I asked, my voice steady despite the fear gnawing at my stomach.

Holmes glanced at the clock on the mantelpiece. "Soon. But first, there are preparations to be made. We cannot enter the labyrinth without understanding its dangers. We must be prepared for anything. I will also send a message to Kovács so he can have his men observe the building of the Freemasons on Podmanicky for Dagian.

With that, we settled for the night. We all tried to sleep, but none of us had much success. I feared the return of the sirens, even though Holmes had shown that they were all a figment of my dreams.

37

LABYRINTH

The sun filtered through the heavy curtains of our suite. The morning light did little to ease the dread that clung to us like the memory of a nightmare.

The previous night's events, the dark whispers in the Red Frog Inn, the revelation of Miss Dagian's murderous treachery, and the ever-looming presence of Dracula had left a pall over our minds, one that the brightest day could not dispel.

Holmes, ever the embodiment of restless energy, was already dressed and standing by the window, peering out over the waking city of Budapest. His silhouette was sharp, a figure of cold logic amid the gathering storm of terror surrounding us.

I stirred, rising from my chair by the hearth, where I had spent much of the early morning in troubled thought. Beside me, Elena remained quiet, her dark eyes focused intently on the map of Castle Hill that lay flat across the table. The lines and markings on the parchment traced the twisting, ancient tunnels that burrowed beneath the city, the labyrinths, a network of passages older than the streets themselves, and our destination this day.

Holmes turned suddenly, his gaze piercing.

"We must move swiftly, Watson, Elena. Time is not a luxury we can afford."

"You believe the tales we heard last night that Dracula is set to meet us within the labyrinths?" I asked.

"It is more than a belief, Watson. It is certain. The information we obtained last night confirms that the tunnels are central to this plot. Miss Dagian's involvement suggests a deeper connection. Dracula is gathering his forces, both living and undead. The labyrinths beneath Castle Hill provide the perfect place for him to do so and remain undisturbed."

"The anarchists are not merely pawns in this game. They are being manipulated, yes, but they serve a purpose, to spread chaos and to fracture order. Dracula's influence has spread like a poison, and the longer we wait, the more powerful he becomes," Elena said, her voice measured but resolute.

Holmes gave a curt nod, already moving toward the door.

"Then we shall not wait any longer."

As we trod down the five floors of the Hotel's grand staircase, I could not shake the feeling that we were descending not merely into the streets of Budapest but into the very depths of darkness itself, into a place where the boundaries between life and death, between light and shadow, were no longer evident.

The streets of Buda were quiet as we made our way toward the entrance to the labyrinths. We moved quickly, our footsteps echoing in the narrow alleyways, the air growing colder as we approached the gate.

Holmes led the way, his sharp eyes scanning every corner, every shadow. Elena and I followed close behind, both of us keenly aware that we were stepping into a place where light and reason held little sway.

An arch of stone standing above a heavily rusted iron gate marked the entrance. A faint, sulfurous smell wafted from the darkness beyond. We could feel the damp air pulsing inside. Holmes paused, his hand resting lightly on the gate's cold iron, before pushing it open with a low creak that sent a shiver down my spine.

We entered the narrow passage. Its walls were slick with moisture. Sporadic locations held carvings of what appeared to be ancient markings and symbols. I held our lantern high above my head as we walked. Strange shapes were cast onto the walls, twisting and contorting them in ways that made the rock seem alive.

"Stay close," Holmes whispered. His voice was barely audible over the dripping water from deep below.

Our sense of unease grew stronger as we ventured further into the labyrinth. The air was thick with the weight of centuries, and the stone beneath our feet was uneven and treacherous. Every turn brought us deeper into the unknown, the passages twisting and narrowing until the earth closed in.

After hours of walking, Holmes raised a hand, signaling us to stop. We stood in a small chamber, the walls lined with alcoves that had once held ancient relics, now long gone. In the center of the chamber lay something far more disturbing, a pile of bones, human remains strewn carelessly across the floor, as though discarded by some malevolent force.

"These are fresh," Elena whispered, her fingers tracing the jagged edge of a broken femur.

"They've been here no more than a few days," I said, kneeling beside Elena.

Holmes' expression hardened, his eyes flicking to the shadows that clung to the chamber's corners. "Dracula's work," he murmured. "Or the work of those who serve him."

I felt a cold sweat across my skin, my hand instinctively reaching for the revolver at my side. "We're not alone down here, Holmes."

"No, we are not alone," Holmes agreed, his voice low.

Then, a faint sound reached our ears. It was the soft shuffle of footsteps, an echo of movement climbing up from the depths. Holmes was already in motion, his lantern swinging wildly as he moved toward the sound.

We followed him down towards the source of the noise. The tunnel narrowed as we advanced. The sound grew louder as we approached, and soon we found ourselves standing in front of a large door. It was slightly ajar, the amber light of a flickering candle visible through the crack.

Holmes raised one hand in a signal for silence. His other rested lightly on the door. He pushed it open with the barest of creaks, revealing a scene that sent a chill through my soul.

The room beyond was vast, the ceiling high and vaulted like some forgotten crypt. In the center of the room stood a makeshift stone altar. It was like the one we had encountered at Chislehurst. Over it was draped a dark cloth surrounded by candles. At the altar knelt a figure, draped in black, a woman, her back to us, her head bowed as though in prayer.

"Miss Dagian," Holmes whispered, his voice tight with tension.

As if sensing our presence, Dagian rose slowly to her feet, turning to face us with a slow, deliberate motion. Her face was pale, her eyes dark and hollow, and there was something in her expression, something cold and inhuman that sent a jolt of terror through me.

"You are too late, Mr. Holmes," she said, her voice a low, hissing whisper. "The time is near. Dracula has awakened, and with him, the Shadow Soul. The dead will rise, and there is nothing you can do to stop it."

Holmes stepped forward, his voice sharp and commanding. "You underestimate me, Miss Dagian. I have faced greater threats than you or Dracula. Your plans will fail."

"We shall see, Mr. Holmes. We shall see," Dagian said. A thin, cruel smile curved her lips.

Before I could react, she turned and disappeared into the shadows, leaving us alone in the chamber. The sound of her footsteps echoed down the tunnels.

38

RESURRECT

The cold, damp air clung to us like a cloak as we descended further into the twisting, oppressive darkness beneath Castle Hill. Narrow stone passages, dripping with moisture and ancient grime, closed around us. The weight of centuries pressed down on us with every step we took. Our Lanterns shone flickering light onto our deepening shadows. Still, they got darker, as though light no longer had any power over them.

"Follow me closely," Holmes said in a whisper.

The detective was deliberate and quiet in his movement. His eyes scanned every inch of the path before us. Elena followed as close as she could in his path. Her face was hard set with a grim determination. I took up the rear, my revolver clutched tightly in hand. We knew that somewhere in the depths of this cursed place lay Dracula's casket, and if we failed to reach it, the horror we had glimpsed would become a reality.

"We must be close," said Elena. She was determined to stop Dracula before he unleashed terror on her home, the city.

"It is near," Holmes murmured, "The chamber is near. I can feel it."

Even I could sense a malignant presence throbbing deeper in the tunnels. Something was pulling us forward.

I ran my hands across the walls, which were full of carvings of a kind I had not seen before. Elena paused momentarily. She, too, ran her fingers over the carvings and gaped at their intricacy.

"These carvings," she whispered. "They must be older than the labyrinth itself. The symbols are of the Shadow Soul, IZ. Kesedes said that this is the source of Dracula's power."

"Then we are on the right path," Holmes replied. "We must be swift. The hour is nearing when his power grows strongest. If we are caught by nightfall, we may not survive."

We pressed forward, and the atmosphere grew thicker. The air became heavy with the unmistakable stench of death and decay. It was then we heard it—faint at first but growing louder with each step, the unmistakable sound of movement. It wasn't the shuffle of shoes or the murmur of voices, but something else, something unnatural, a low, rasping noise that sent a chill through our bones.

"What can that be?" asked Elena.

"Dracula's hordes," he said quietly. "They are near. Prepare yourselves."

Holmes stopped abruptly, his hand raised in warning. I felt my heart pound in my chest as I tightened my grip on the revolver, the weight suddenly feeling insignificant against the terrible force that awaited us. Elena drew her dagger, her eyes gleaming in the lantern light. The sound grew closer and closer.

Then, from the darkness ahead, they emerged. Pale figures, their skin drawn tight over their skeletal frames. Skulls with empty hollows stumbled toward us in a grotesque, shambling procession. Tattered military uniforms hung from their emaciated bodies. Large gold rings imprinted with the double-headed eagle sat on their fingers as a mark of their allegiance. The soldiers moved with a dreadful purpose, their twisted forms lurching forward, grasping for our flesh.

"Watson!" Holmes called, and I fired into the first of them, the sharp crack of the gunshot echoing through the tunnel. The creature collapsed in a heap of dust and bone, but a second soon took its place. They pushed forward without fear, driven by some unseen will.

Elena flung herself forward with deadly grace, her dagger slicing through the air as she dispatched one of the creatures with a swift strike to the throat. Its skull tumbled from its spine. Holmes, ever precise, dodged and parried with the skill of a man who had long since mastered the art of the stick. But still, they came, their numbers seemingly endless.

"To the chamber!" Holmes shouted above the din. "We must reach the chamber!"

We fought through the horde, the narrow passage forcing us to battle in close quarters, and the stench of decay was overpowering. Every shot and strike was met with another of the creatures, their blank faces twisted in silent, eternal fury. But we did not falter, our resolve unbroken even as the odds seemed insurmountable.

At last, we broke through into a wider space, the very chamber we had sought. Dracula's resting place.

The room was vast, the stone walls rising above us, the ceiling lost in shadow. And at the center of the chamber, upon a raised dais, lay the coffin, its black surface gleaming like obsidian in the dim light of our lanterns. Around it stood more of the undead, their still forms guarding their master's sanctuary with unwavering loyalty.

As Holmes approached the dais, a voice, cold and sharp as a blade, cut through the chamber.

"You are too late, Holmes."

Dracula emerged from the shadows beyond the casket, his tall, gaunt figure as imposing as ever. His eyes burned with a terrible light, his lips curling into a cruel smile. His long, black hair fell in waves around his pale face. His fingers were long and slender, spread like the claws of some predatory bird. There was no mistaking the power he held, the force of IZ flowing through him like a dark current.

Holmes froze, his sharp gaze locked with the Count's. "You will not unleash this horror upon the world," he said, his voice filled with cold fury. "Your plans end here, Dracula."

Dracula's smile widened, revealing the sharp points of his fangs.

"You think you can stop me?" he hissed. "You, who are bound by the limits of mortality? I have lived for centuries, and my power only grows stronger. You cannot kill what death itself cannot claim."

With terrifying speed, Dracula moved. Before we could react, the Count stepped back into the shadows, his form dissolving into the darkness. In a moment, he was gone, leaving only the crumbling remnants of his altar. We stood in shock, the reality of his escape sinking in. But our determination to stop him grew stronger, our minds racing to devise a new plan.

We stood silently, the weight of what had just occurred settling over us like a heavy cloak. The undead, deprived of Dracula's control, collapsed to the ground, their bodies turning to dust in the still air.

Holmes approached the dais, his face grim as he examined the remains of the coffin. "He has escaped," he said quietly. "But he has left something behind."

I stepped closer, peering over Holmes' shoulder as he pulled a folded sheet of parchment from the coffin's remains. The paper was old and yellowed with age, but its markings were unmistakable.

"It is a map of Europe," Holmes explained, tracing the lines with his finger. "These marks indicate places of burial, ancient sites where Dracula has been harvesting the dead."

"He's raising an army," Elena said, her face still pale from the encounter.

"Indeed. This map shows the locations of graves he has already disturbed. But there are more sites he has yet to reach," said Holmes grimly.

"Then what must we do, Holmes?" I said as a shiver ran down my spine.

Holmes turned to face us, his eyes gleaming with fierce determination. "We must stop him. We must have the authorities find these sites before he does, and destroy any remnants of his power. Dracula has escaped us today, but his plans have been revealed. And we now have the means to thwart him."

With the map in hand, we left the chamber, the dark corridors of the labyrinths closing behind us as we returned to the surface. The fight was far from over, but for the first time, we had a weapon against the darkness that had pursued us.

And as we stepped into the light of day, I knew that we could not rest until we had removed this threat from Dracula's grip.

39

ON FIRE

The sky over Budapest was an appropriate reflection of the turmoil beneath it. Dark clouds roiled above, heavy with the threat of rain, while the cold air seemed to cling to the skin like the breath of some unseen predator.

For now, Dracula had escaped, but in doing so, he had left us the key to his defeat: a parchment, yellowed with age and marked with dark symbols, and a map detailing the locations throughout Europe of the cemeteries and catacombs he had targeted.

Holmes sat at the table in our suite at the Hotel Hungaria. The map spread before him. His sharp, calculating gaze swept over the inked lines and circles, marking cities, towns, and forgotten places where Dracula had begun his grim work. We had messaged

Inspector Kovács to attend our suite as soon as possible to view our findings.

Elena stood by the window, her figure bathed in the faint morning light, arms crossed in quiet contemplation. I could not help but feel the cold fingers of dread creeping up my spine. We were racing against time, and the stakes had never been higher.

Holmes spoke at last, his voice steady but tinged with the task's urgency. "This map," he said, his finger tracing a line across Europe, "reveals far more than Dracula's resting places. It shows a pattern, a network of graves that stretches from Paris to Constantinople and beyond. These are not random sites, Watson. He has been methodical, strategic."

I leaned forward, examining the parchment more closely. The names of towns and cities leaped out at me; Paris, Venice, Berlin, Bucharest. All are marked with the same ominous symbols. "What is his purpose, Holmes?" I asked. "Why disturb these graves?"

Elena, who had remained silent until now, turned to face us, her expression grim. "He is raising an army," she said quietly. "The dead that lie in these places, soldiers, warriors, men of violence, they are the instruments of Dracula's war. He is preparing them to rise, to fight once more. And when they do, they will be under his command, bound to him through the power of IZ."

Holmes nodded. "Indeed. The shadow soul, IZ, gives him dominion over these corpses. They are not merely reanimated bodies, they are soldiers imbued with a dark force that makes them almost invincible. If we do not stop him, they will sweep across Europe like a plague, leaving death and destruction in their wake."

A shiver ran through me at the thought. "But how can we stop Dracula, Holmes? We cannot be everywhere at once. The burial sites are scattered across the continent."

Holmes tapped the map with his finger, his gaze narrowing. "We may not need to be. If we can identify the key site. The place where he intends to raise the largest number of undead, we can cut off his power at the source. He cannot raise his army without certain rituals and certain preparations. We must disrupt those before they are completed."

"And the anarchists?" asked Elena.

"Dracula is using them as pawns. Their acts of violence and their unrest create the perfect cover for him to perform his rituals. No one notices a few disturbed graves when cities are on fire."

"Then Boschetti must be stopped as well," I said. "If he is allowed to continue, Dracula will have the perfect opportunity to complete his work."

"Precisely, Watson. Boschetti is the key to this. We must find him and sever the connection between him and Dracula before it is too late. The anarchists are scattered across the continent, but they have a central hub right here, in Budapest. That is where we must begin. Our resolve was unshakable, our determination unwavering.

Then there was a knock at the door. I moved to open it while Holmes and Elena stood ready.

"Who is it?" I asked.

"Kovács," came the reply.

"I'm delighted you came, Inspector."

"Good to meet you, Mr. Holmes. Your message tells of some urgency."

"Yes, we have found the meeting place of Boschetti and his anarchists."

"Where?"

Elena moved to join us, her hand resting on the hilt of the dagger she had carried since we first ventured into the labyrinths. "We know that the anarchists have been meeting in Ferencváros, near the docks. There, we will find Boschetti and, with him, the link to Dracula."

"How did you come across such information?" Kovács asked.

"We have good sources."

"I have been looking for this group for months. Why should I believe you?"

"Whether you believe us or not, inspector, is not the point. We are going to this address, and we will confront them. It is up to you whether you bring your forces to bear."

"I will organize a small party to meet you there, Mr. Holmes."

Holmes nodded, his expression grim. "Then we have no time to lose. We go to Ferencváros at once."

40

SHADOWS

The Ferencváros district was a labyrinth of narrow streets and dark alleys, its warehouses and factories looming over us like silent sentinels. The scent of the Danube hung heavy in the air, mixed with the acrid smoke of industry. It was a place of shadows where the law held little sway, and danger lurked around every corner. The perfect hiding place for men like Boschetti.

We moved cautiously through the maze of streets, our eyes scanning every shadow, every figure that passed us by. Holmes led the way with the same unerring sense of purpose that had guided us through so many dark places before. His hand rested lightly on the pocket where the map was concealed, his keen mind undoubtedly working through the details of what would come.

At last, we reached a small, unassuming warehouse, its windows dark, its doors shut tight. From the outside, it appeared abandoned, but there was no mistaking the faint sounds of voices and movement from within. Holmes signaled for us to stop, his eyes narrowing as he observed the building.

"This is the place," he whispered. "Boschetti is inside."

We crept closer, the weight of what would come pressing down upon us. Like the undead, the anarchists were soldiers in a war they scarcely understood. But where the undead were mindless, Boschetti's men were driven by fervor, believing they could topple the very fabric of society. And in their desperation, they had allied themselves with a force far darker than they could comprehend.

Holmes gestured for Elena to join Kovacs and his men and sit near the side entrance while he and I approached the main door. With a swift motion, he drew a small lock-picking tool from his coat and set to work. The door creaked open with a soft groan, and we slipped inside.

The warehouse's interior was dimly lit by a few flickering lanterns, casting long shadows across the crates and barrels that filled the space. In the center of the room, a group of seven men sat huddled around a table, their voices low and urgent. Among them, unmistakable in his bearing and presence, was Green…

Holmes moved with the silence of a predator, his sharp eyes fixed on Green. We drew closer, hidden by the darkness, until we could hear their conversation.

"It is almost time," Green said, his voice filled with conviction. "The Count has given us the means to bring Europe to its knees. When the dead rise, no government or king will be able to stand against us."

One of the men shifted uneasily. "But what of the Count himself? Can we trust him?"

Green's eyes gleamed with fanaticism. "Dracula is a force of nature. He cannot be controlled, but he can be harnessed. And when the time comes, we will wield his power for our own ends."

Holmes' voice cut through the darkness like a blade. "You are a fool, Green."

The anarchists leaped to their feet, their hands reaching for weapons. Still, Holmes stepped forward into the light, his expression cold and unyielding.

"Dracula has no interest in your revolution," Holmes continued. "He is using you, as he has used so many others before. And when he is finished, you will be nothing more than dust beneath his feet."

Green turned. "You say, Green, Mr. Holmes?" and crackled with laughter.

"Yes, Mr. Green, the Orient Express, we met there. You were involved in the murder of Guinness. You and Miss Dagian together."

"Of course. Mr. Guinness, a clever spy he turned out to be. Didn't he? But Mr. Holmes, you are wrong in your deduction. A quite remarkable event if true by itself, wouldn't you say?"

"I know you killed him, Green."

"You are correct, Mr. Holmes. I hit him at the back of the head," Green said, then raised his hand to show the gold ring in position on his finger. "Then Dagian very kindly pushed her little hatpin slowly into his heart. Very efficient, don't you think?"

"I am correct!"

"Not entirely, Mr. Holmes. You see, I am not Mr. Green; I am...Boschetti!" Boschetti sneered.

"You do not understand, Holmes. The world is already crumbling. We are simply hastening its fall. And when the old order is gone, a new one will rise, one built in our image."

Holmes' eyes flashed with anger. "And in the meantime, you unleash a plague of death upon the world. How many innocent lives will be lost before you realize you are nothing more than a pawn in Dracula's game?"

Before Boschetti could respond, the door behind us burst open, and Kovács and his men rushed forward.

Elena stepped into the room, her dagger drawn, her face fierce with determination.

"It ends here, Boschetti," she said, her voice low and steady. "You will not raise Dracula's army. We will stop you."

Boschetti's sneer faltered, and for the first time, I saw a flicker of uncertainty in his eyes. But it was too late. Kovács moved swiftly, his hand closing around Boschetti's wrist, disarming him instantly. The police had surrounded the building. The anarchist leader struggled, but it was clear that the tide had turned.

"We will stop him," Holmes said quietly, his gaze fixed on Boschetti. "And you will answer for what you have done."

As Kovács and his force bound Boschetti and his men, I felt a sense of grim satisfaction. We had severed one of Dracula's most powerful alliances, and in doing so, we had struck a blow against his plans. But the war was far from over. The burial sites still called to us, their secrets waiting to be uncovered.

41

BATTLE

The night was black as pitch, the streets of Budapest swallowed by a darkness that felt not of this world. The heavy clouds above blocked the moon, leaving the city beneath them to writhe in shadows. The air itself felt unnatural, thick with dread and anticipation, as if the city knew what was coming, what was already unfolding beneath its very foundations.

We gathered again at the Hotel Hungaria, barely an hour after our latest discovery. Ever the picture of composed intensity, Holmes stood near the window, his eyes scanning the gloom beyond, his mind working through possibilities and outcomes, each one more dire than the last. Elena, her dark gaze steady, was seated near the hearth, her hand resting lightly on the hilt of her dagger. I sat nearby, the weight of our situation pressing upon me like a leaden cloak.

And then there came the knock at the door. A rapid, urgent rap echoed through the dimly lit room.

Holmes turned sharply, crossing the room in swift, deliberate strides. As he opened the door, the flickering lamplight from the hallway revealed two figures standing there: Inspector Kovács, his massive frame barely fitting through the threshold, and at his side, a boy, no more than thirteen, with bright eyes and a familiar, resolute expression. Beside him, a pointer dog's large, muscular form stood poised, alert, and ready.

"Quincey!" I exclaimed,

"I couldn't stay behind," Quincey said, his voice steady but youthful determination clear. "Not when I knew what was happening. I had to help. The telegrams from Mr. Holmes confirmed the matter. And Earl Chesterfield granted special leave from the barracks.

At his side, Prince, the pointer dog, stood with his nose lifted toward the air, sensing the night's unrest. He let out a low growl, his dark eyes gleaming in the dim light.

Holmes smiled, though it was a smile tinged with gravity. "Your father would be proud, Quincey," he said, his voice firm but laced with approval. "But you must understand the danger we face. This is not a fight for the faint of heart."

"I know, Mr. Holmes. But Prince and I, we're ready. You know that we've faced worse things before. We can help," the boy pulled out his kukri and flashed it around his head.

"There it is!" I shouted in support.

Inspector Kovács stepped forward, his gruff voice cutting through the moment. "We've brought reinforcements, Mr. Holmes. My men are ready, but we'll need every advantage we can get. We received word that Miss Dagian has been seen near the Kerepesi Cemetery, where we suspect Dracula is raising his army."

We explained what Kovács and his men needed to do to upgrade their weapons. After a brief moment of disbelief, we managed the Inspector to ensure everything was prepared.

"We don't have a moment to lose. We go now," said Holmes.

The streets leading to Kerepesi Cemetery were eerily silent, the lamps dimmed by the oppressive weight of the night. Our group moved swiftly, led by Inspector Kovács and his police team, their lanterns flickering against the gloom. Quincey kept close to me, his hand resting on the thick fur of Prince, who moved with a predatory grace, his nose leading the way. Holmes strode ahead, his sharp eyes scanning every shadow, while Elena, ever watchful, followed close behind.

As we neared the cemetery gates, the air grew colder

and sharper. The stones beneath our feet seemed to vibrate with the dark energy that pulsed from the earth. There was no mistaking it. We were close to the source of Dracula's power. The graves beyond the gate seemed to shift in the dim light, their shapes distorted, as though the dead themselves were preparing to rise.

Holmes stopped suddenly, his hand raised for silence. We stood at the cemetery's threshold, the wrought-iron gates looming before us like the mouth of some great beast, ready to devour all who entered. From somewhere within the fog-shrouded darkness, we could hear it. A low, rhythmic sound, like the beating of distant wings.

"The undead are stirring," Holmes murmured, his voice grim. "We must be prepared."

Kovács gave a sharp nod, signaling his men to spread out, their hands tightening on their weapons. Quincey crouched beside Prince, the dog's body tense, his ears perked, ready to act at the first sign of danger.

Holmes turned to me, his eyes locking onto mine with a fierce intensity. "Watson, stay close. Miss Dagian will be here. And with her, Dracula's servants."

We stepped through the gates, our lanterns casting weak, flickering light across the gravestones and mausoleums that filled the cemetery. The fog hung thick, swirling around us as we moved deeper into the heart of the necropolis, where the ground seemed to pulse with dark energy.

Then, from the mist, they appeared.

Hands and fingers scrabbled and clawed at the earth, first arms and heads, then torsos. Once their legs cleared the earth, they formed ranks and began to march with an unnatural grace. Their movements began as jerky and stiff, but soon became organized. They seemed to be filled with an unholy strength. Moving as one, they came towards where we stood. Each soldier was wearing the double-headed eagle held within the golden ring.

"Fire!" Inspector Kovács shouted, and his men unleashed a volley of gunfire, the sharp crack of their rifles cutting through the stillness. The bullets struck the undead, but they did not fall. Instead, they staggered, their twisted forms barely slowed by the onslaught.

Holmes moved swiftly, drawing a vial of holy water from his coat and flinging it toward the nearest creature. The water sizzled as it struck the ghoul's flesh, burning through it like acid. The beast let out a horrible, inhuman wail before collapsing into a pile of dust.

"Watson, now!" Holmes called, and I raised my revolver, firing into the mass of creatures that surrounded us. Elena was at my side, her dagger flashing in the dim light as she struck down one of the undead with a swift, precise blow to the neck.

Quincey's determined face gave a sharp whistle, and

Prince leaped into action. The dog's powerful body crashed into one of the undead, knocking it to the ground. The creature shrieked as Prince tore into it, his jaws clamping ferociously.

But even as we fought, the fog thickened, and through the swirling mist, a figure emerged. It was Miss Dagian.

Her pale face was as cold and unfeeling as ever, her dark eyes gleaming with malevolence. She stood at the far end of the cemetery, her hands raised, directing the movements of the undead like a conductor orchestrating a macabre symphony.

"Holmes!" I shouted, pointing toward the figure in the distance.

Holmes' eyes narrowed, his jaw tightening. "Dagian. She's controlling them. We must stop her, or the dead will overwhelm us."

We fought our way through the horde of the raised soldiers, the creatures closing in from all sides, their cold hands grasping at us with terrifying strength. But we pressed forward, our movements swift and precise, driven by the knowledge that to falter here would mean death.

As we neared Miss Dagian, she let out a low, cruel laugh, her voice carrying through the fog like the tolling of a bell.

"You are too late, Holmes," she hissed. "Dracula's

army will rise, and all of Europe will fall under his shadow."

Holmes did not hesitate. He drew a silver stake from his coat and hurled it toward her with a single, fluid motion. The stake flew through the air, striking her squarely in the chest. Dagian let out a gasp, her eyes widening in shock as the silver burned through her flesh.

The control she held over the undead faltered. The creatures around us staggered, their movements growing sluggish and disjointed.

"Now!" Holmes shouted. "We must destroy them before they regain their strength."

With renewed vigor, we attacked, striking down the remaining undead. One by one, the soldiers fell, their bodies crumbling into dust.

At last, the cemetery was still.

We stood in silence, our breaths heavy, the weight of what we had just endured pressing down upon us. Dagian lay motionless on the ground, her pale form twisted and broken, her dark eyes staring lifelessly at the sky.

Holmes knelt beside her, his expression hard. "Dracula may have escaped us tonight," he said quietly, "but his servant is no more."

I looked around at the bodies of the fallen undead, their twisted forms reduced to ash and dust. We had won a battle, but the war was far from over.

Holmes rose, his gaze turning to the distant horizon. "Dracula will return, Watson. And when he does, we must be ready."

Acknowledgement

Big thanks to Ellissa and to the rest of my amazing Freeman family, Deanna, Anisha and Lukas.

Thank you to the Flourish Group for all that you do.

Books By This Author

Sherlock & Dracula - Lifeblood (book 1)

The first book of this series is set seven years after Dracula's apparent demise at the hands of Jonathan Harker, and his five compatriots in the forests of the Carpathian Mountains. Sherlock Holmes is asked by Mina Harker to help track down what she believes is the returning vampire before he takes his revenge. But she may be too late. Can Sherlock and Dr. Watson find the lair of Dracula located somewhere in Victorian London before vengeance is served. www.sherlockdracula.com for more information, maps, evidence and journals.

Sherlock & Dracula - Imperial (book 2)

The case of Sherlock Holmes & Dracula: 'Imperial,' follows on from the events of Sherlock Holmes & Dracula: 'Lifeblood.' Events take the team to the small London town of Chislehurst, once the abode of Napoleon III, where a mysterious murder grips the community in terror. Desperate for answers, local Detective Hopkins turns to the legendary detective Sherlock Holmes. As Holmes delves deeper into the chilling case, he uncovers a labyrinthine underground web of secrets, lies, and dark desires lurking beneath the surface of the seemingly idyllic town. With each step closer to the truth, Holmes discovers connections to Chislehurst's haunted past and the resurfacing of his nemesis, the infamous Count Dracula.

Frankenstein 2035

It's 2035. Beta, a young Austrian scientist, seeks a cure for her only remaining family member, her disabled brother. She understands she his is only hope. After being handed an old recipe for creating life, she accepts an invitation from a mysterious group to join other researchers at an arctic station in Nunavut, Canada. Meanwhile, in that same location, divers pull something, preserved by the almost freezing water, from a wreck which has lain at the bottom of the arctic ocean for more than 200 years.

Upon the Generation of Life - *by Victor Frankenstein*

A short story companion to Frankenstein or the Modern Prometheus by Mary Shelley, and Frankenstein 2035 by Kev Freeman. The journal written by Victor Frankenstein recording his final experiments leading to the recipe and creation of life.

Whitby Rock

An action-filled murder-mystery detective novel describes a crime that wraps itself though time and geographic location, everyday events happen for no reason other than to become remarkable and connect to a thread of synchronicity. Enjoy a thrilling tale of mystery, murder, robbery, and suspense that will engage you from start to finish.

LUCY & The True Grimoire

This fantasy/horror/detective Novelette is the prequel to the case of 'LUCY RISING' (the first book in the Birch and Kane detective series, first two chapters included). The personal journal of tattooist Greg Bentley who, after a late-night visit by a mysterious young woman, becomes embroiled in a fantasy world in modern-day London. The document, later taken into evidence, tells the story of how the strange 'Lucy' uses her knowledge of angels, obtained through the book of The True Grimoire, to call upon the 18 Angels in service of her Master. The True Grimoire is the handbook of magic. A manual of incantations and methodologies, which set in place the manifestation of energies willing to participate in the expansion of the dark kingdom.